Dear parents, caregivers, and educators:

If you want to get your child excited about reading, you've come to the right place! Ready-to-Read *GRAPHICS* is the perfect launchpad for emerging graphic novel readers.

All Ready-to-Read *GRAPHICS* books include the following:

★ **A how-to guide to reading graphic novels for first-time readers**

★ **Easy-to-follow panels to support reading comprehension**

★ **Accessible vocabulary to build your child's reading confidence**

★ **Compelling stories that star your child's favorite characters**

★ **Fresh, engaging illustrations that provide context and promote visual literacy**

Wherever your child may be on their reading journey, Ready-to-Read *GRAPHICS* will make them giggle, gasp, and want to keep reading more.

Blast off on this starry adventure . . . a universe of graphic novel reading awaits!

e a OO EMERGENCY

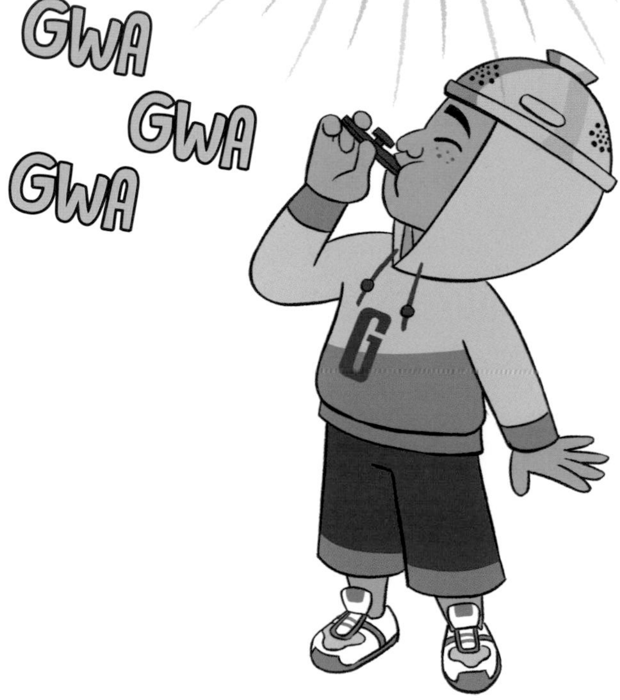
GWA
GWA
GWA

Ready-to-Read *GRAPHICS*

Simon Spotlight
New York London Toronto Sydney New Delhi

For Ari, who is always prepared for a
kazoo emergency, and Hazel, who sent
me a kazoo duck, which brought me luck
—H. E. Y. S.

To my wife and daughter, who put up
with my unorthodox ways, and to
everyone who thinks about and sees
the world differently—keep being you!
The world needs you.
—S. S.

SIMON SPOTLIGHT
An imprint of Simon & Schuster Children's Publishing Division
1230 Avenue of the Americas, New York, New York 10020
This Simon Spotlight edition May 2023
Text copyright © 2023 by Heidi E. Y. Stemple
Illustrations copyright © 2023 by Selom Sunu
SIMON SPOTLIGHT, READY-TO-READ, and colophon are registered
trademarks of Simon & Schuster, Inc.
For information about special discounts for bulk purchases, please contact Simon & Schuster
Special Sales at 1-866-506-1949 or business@simonandschuster.com.
Manufactured in China 1222 SCP
2 4 6 8 10 9 7 5 3 1
This book has been cataloged with the Library of Congress.
ISBN 978-1-6659-2004-9 (hc)
ISBN 978-1-6659-2003-2 (pbk)
ISBN 978-1-6659-2005-6 (ebook)

CONTENTS

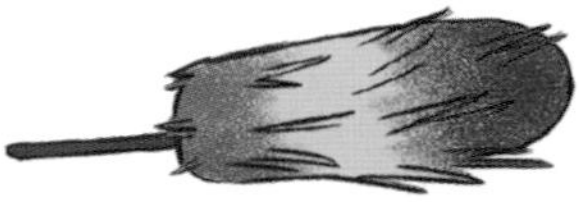

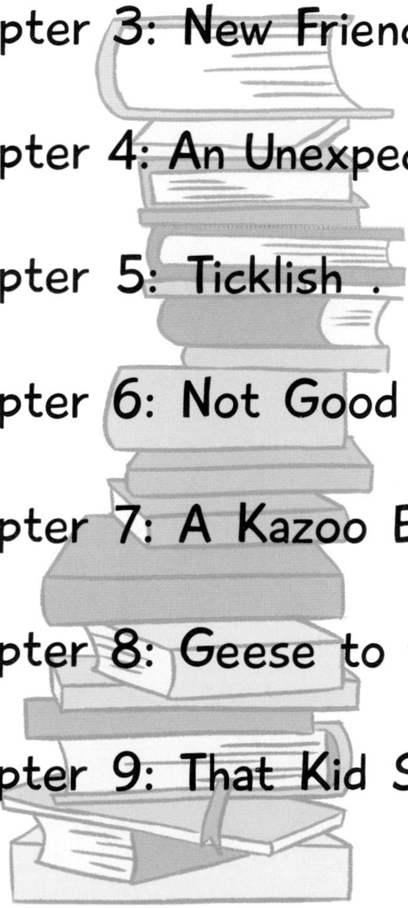

HOW TO READ THIS BOOK

This is Gregory James. He is here to give you some tips on reading this book!

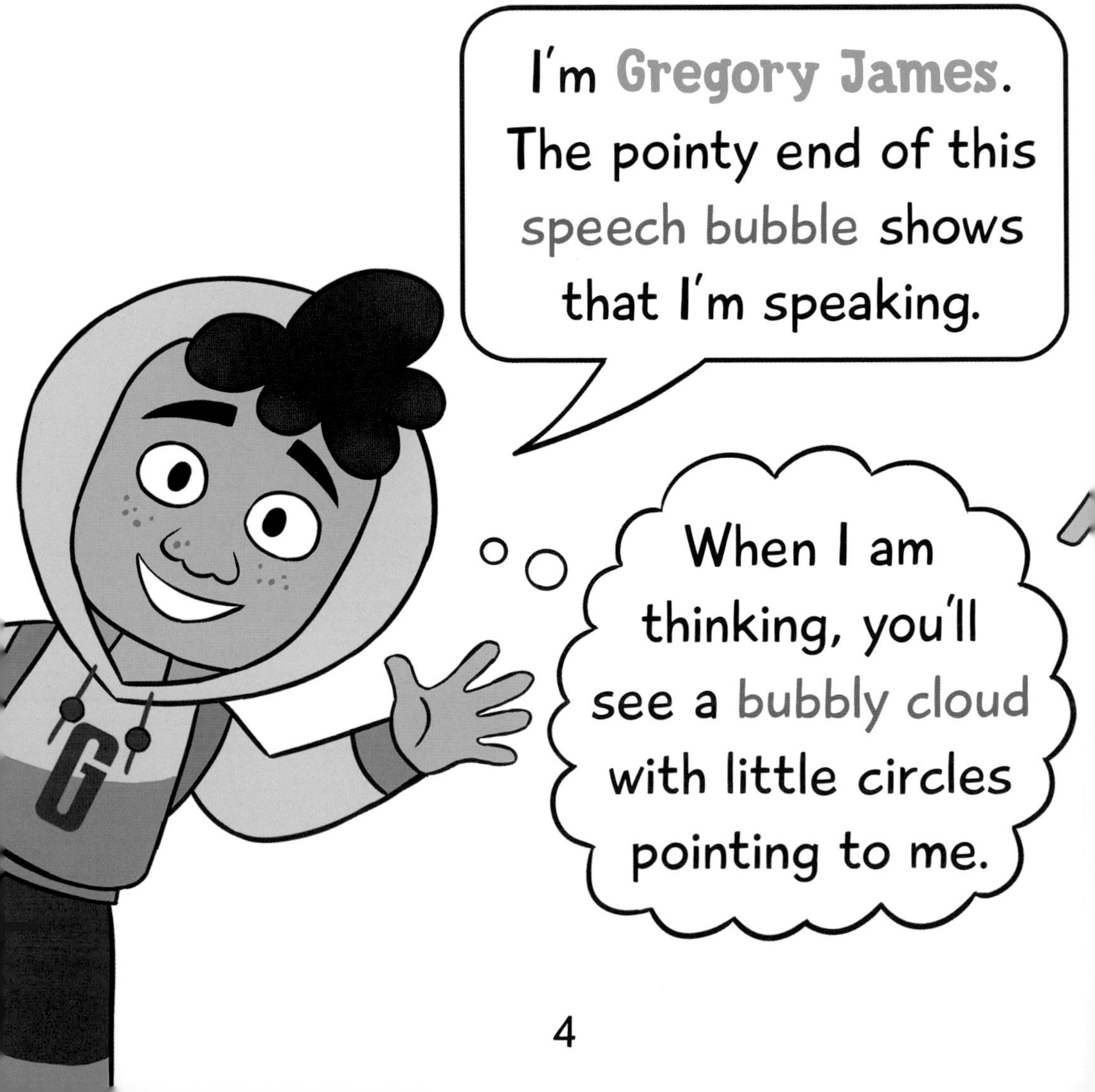
I'm Gregory James. The pointy end of this speech bubble shows that I'm speaking.
When I am thinking, you'll see a bubbly cloud with little circles pointing to me.
G

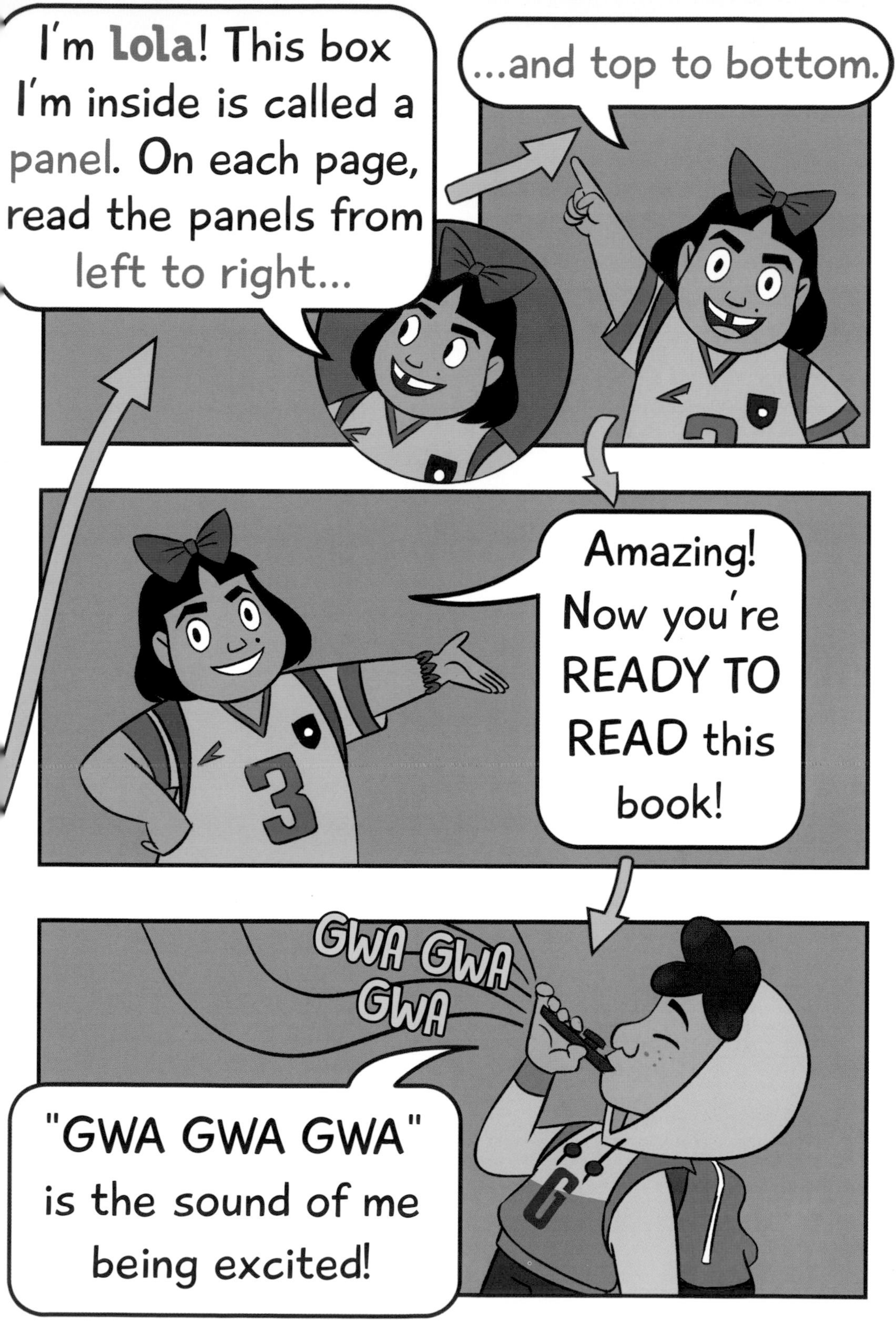
I'm **Lola**! This box I'm inside is called a panel. On each page, read the panels from left to right...
...and top to bottom.
Amazing! Now you're READY TO READ this book!
GWA GWA
GWA
"GWA GWA GWA" is the sound of me being excited!

CHAPTER 1: GREGORY JAMES

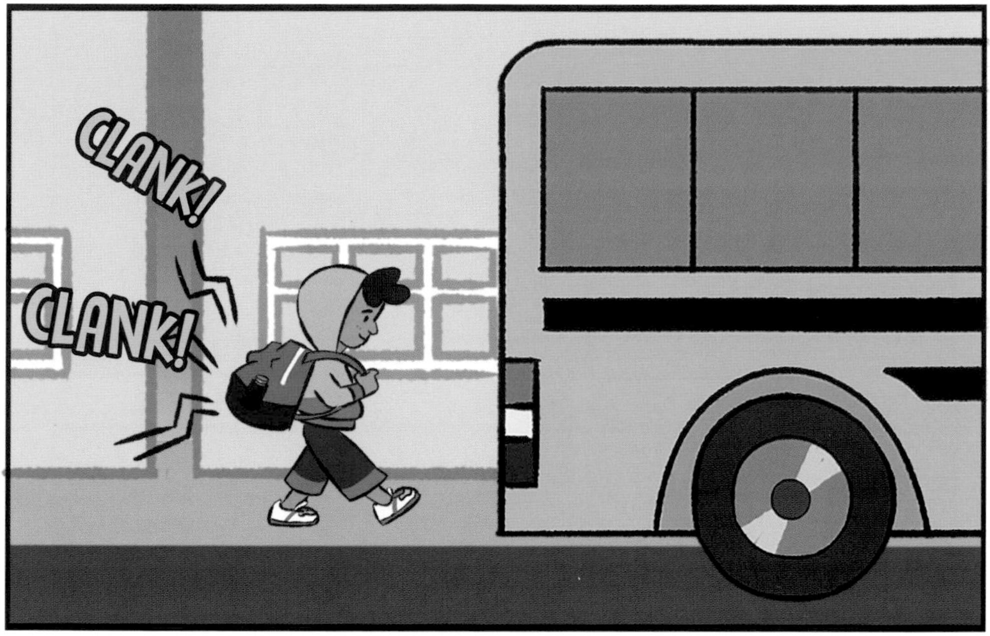
CLANK!
CLANK!

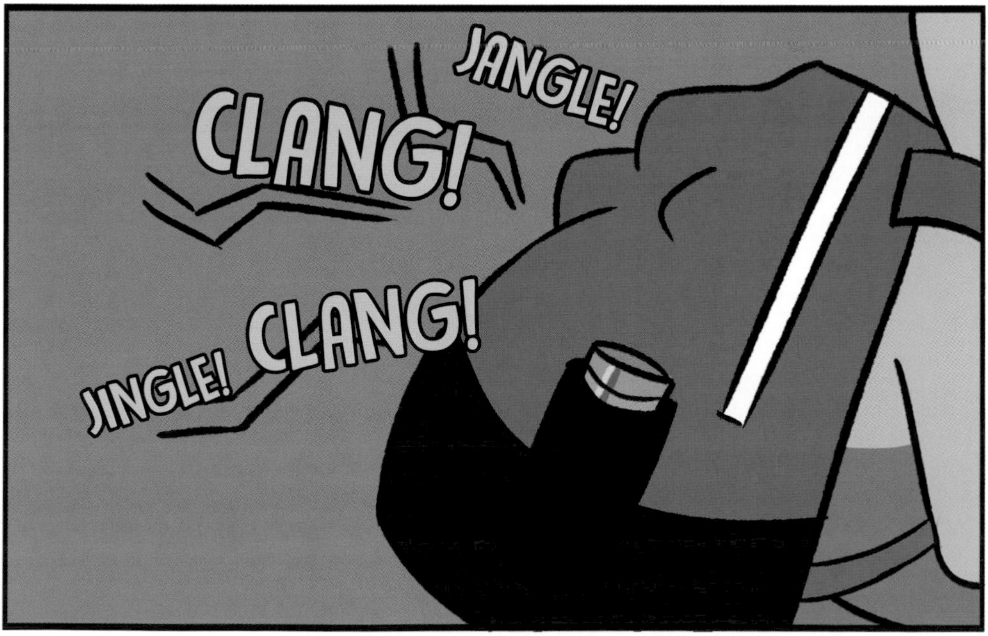
JANGLE!
CLANG!
JINGLE! CLANG!

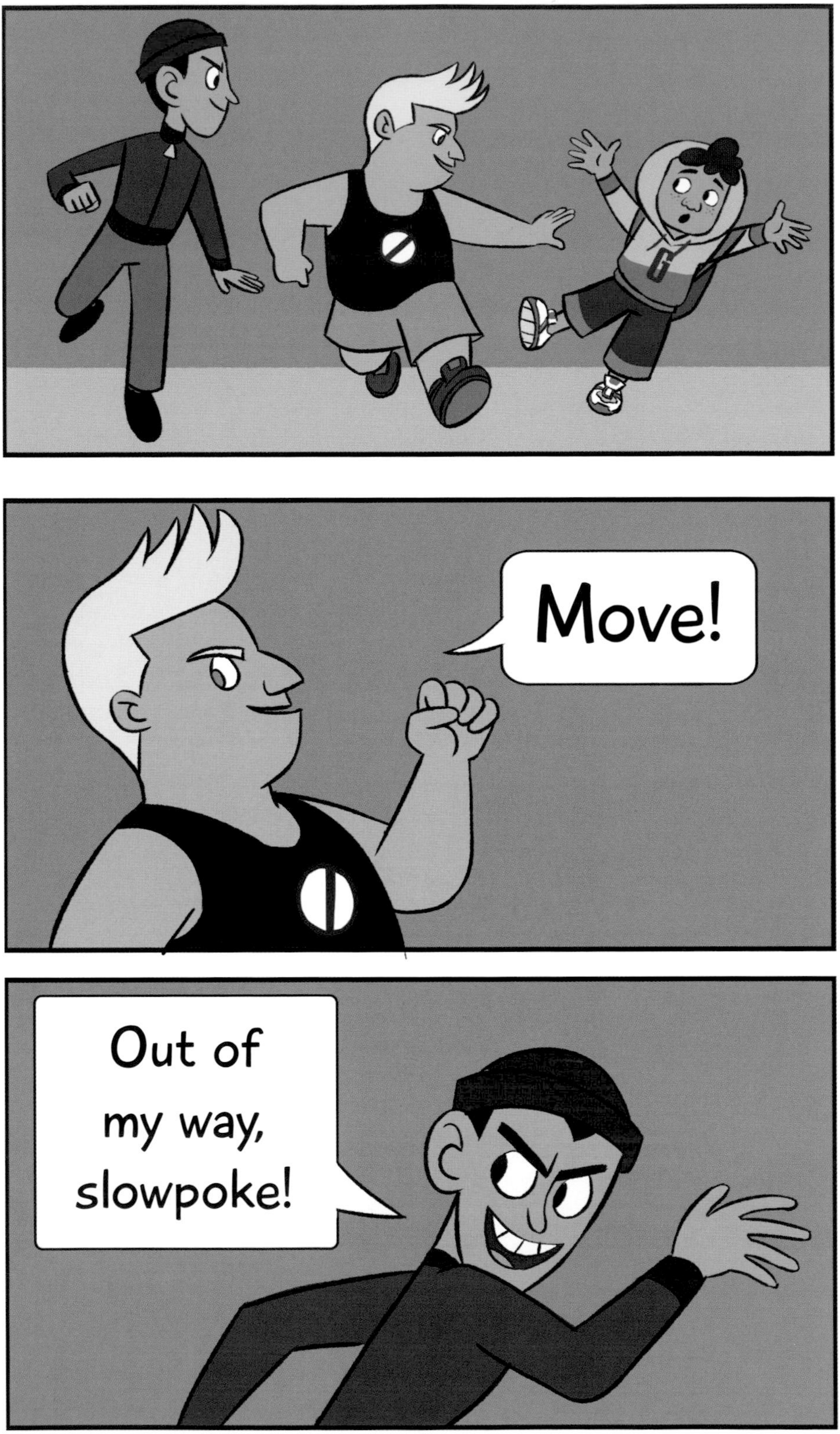
Move!
Out of my way, slowpoke!

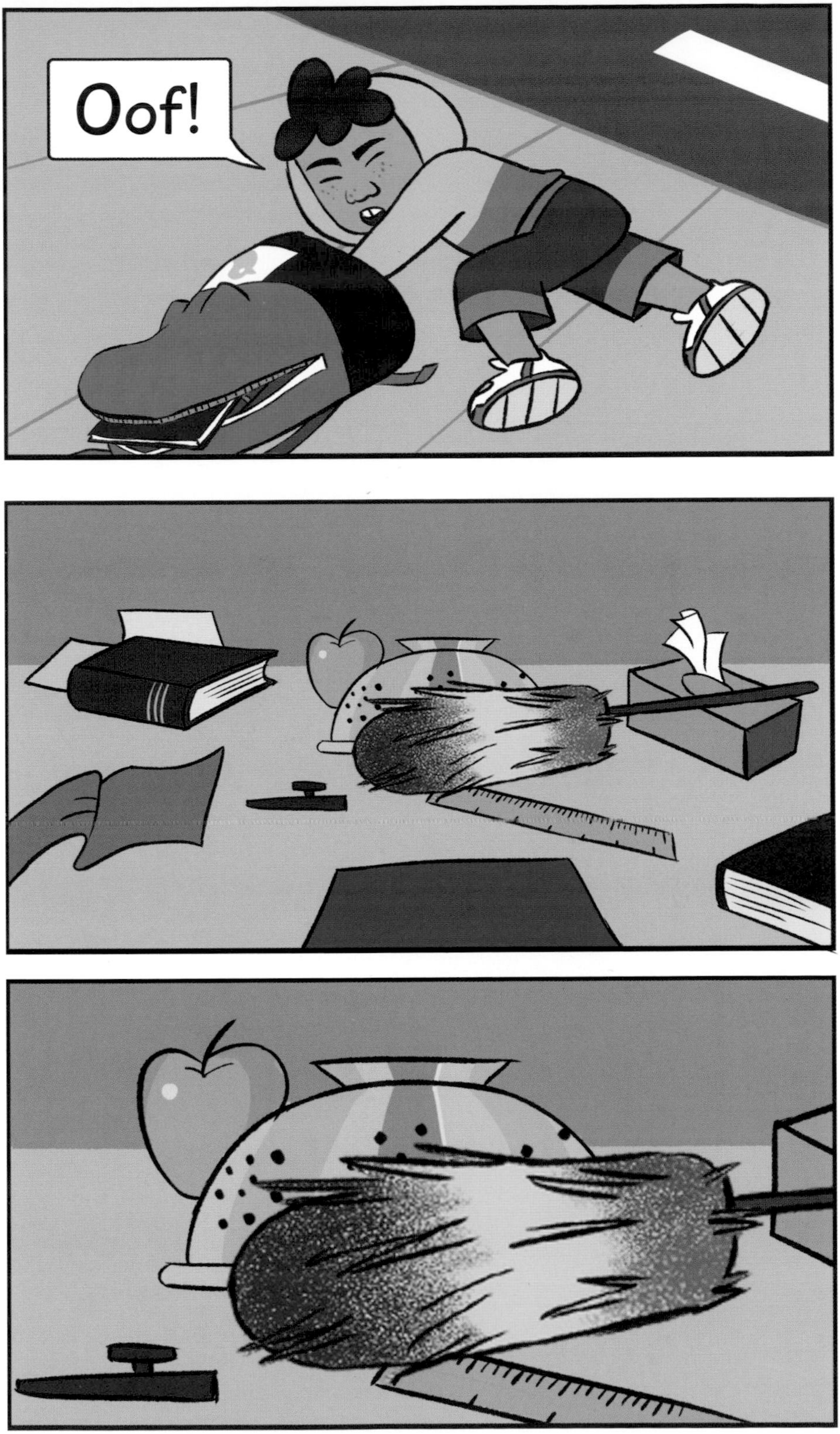
Oof!

CHAPTER 2: LOLA

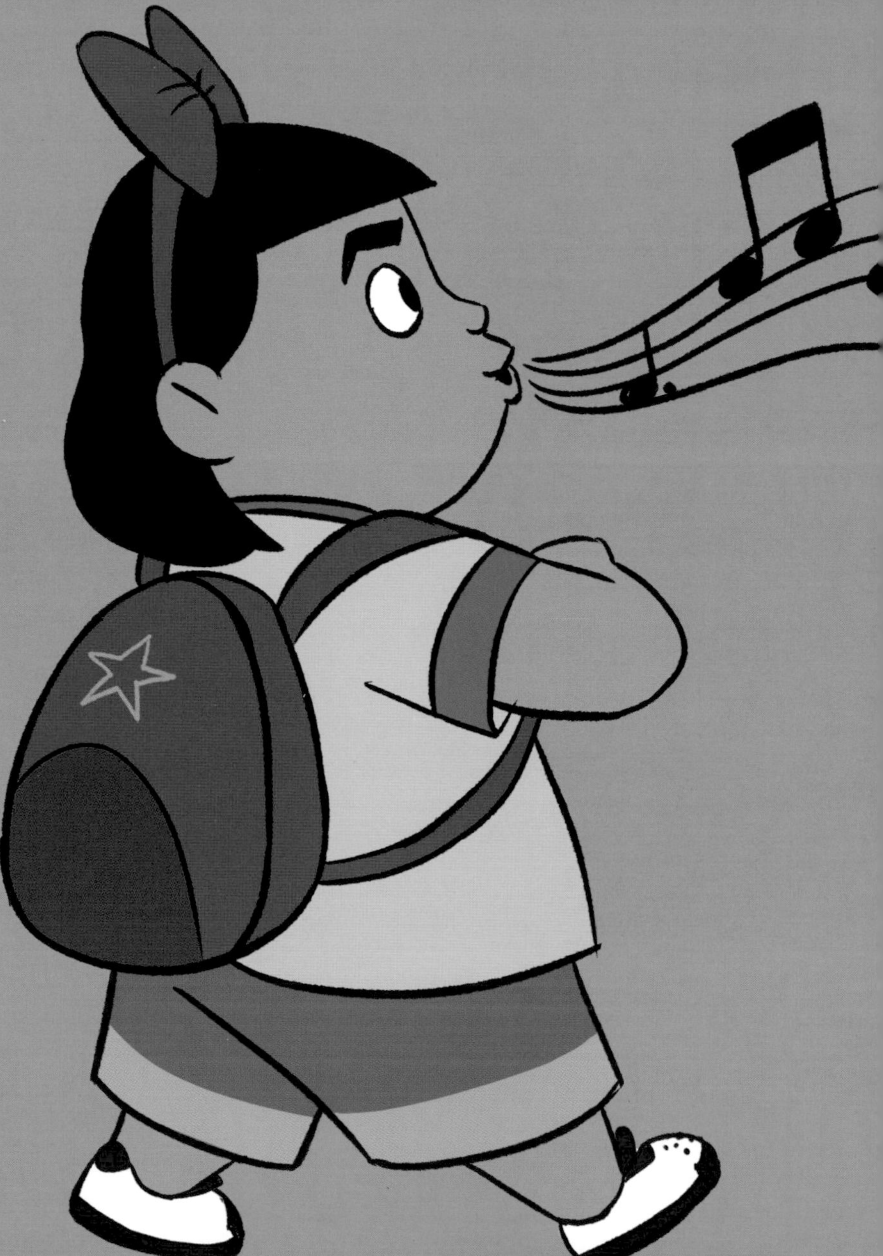

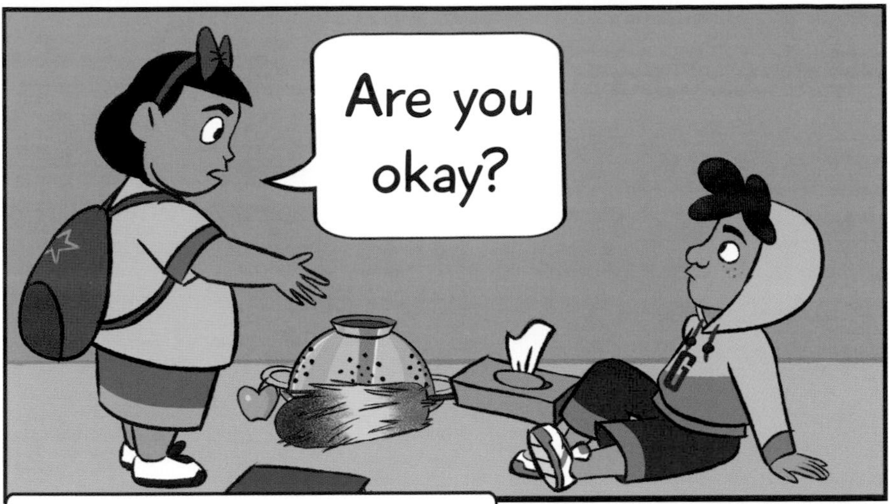
Are you okay?

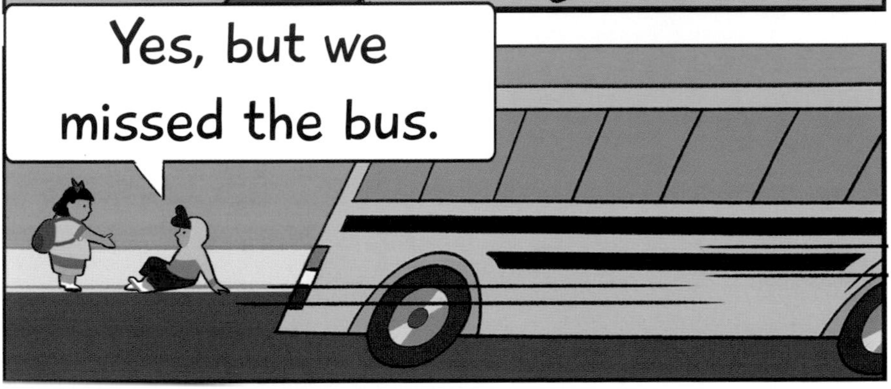
Yes, but we missed the bus.

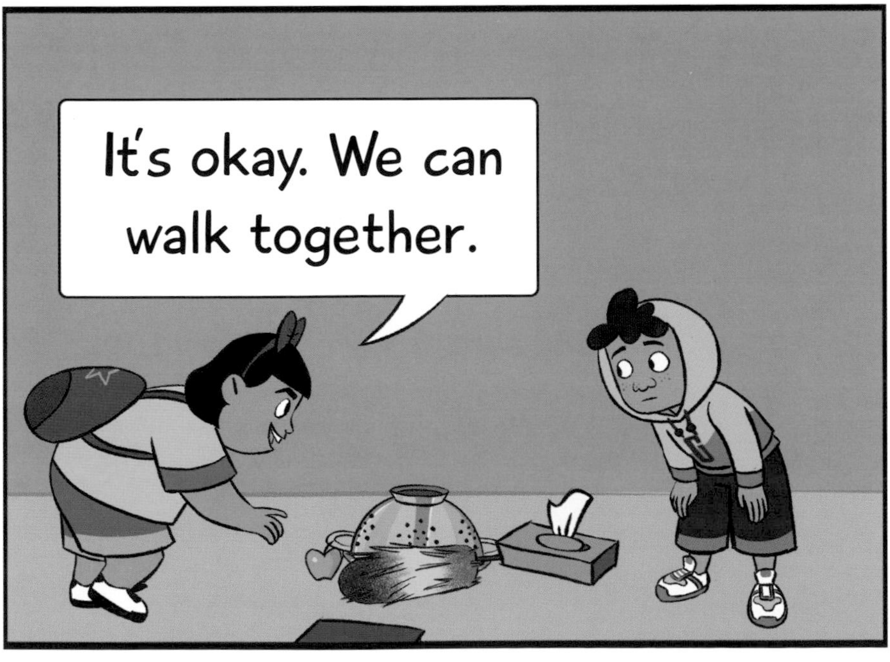
It's okay. We can walk together.

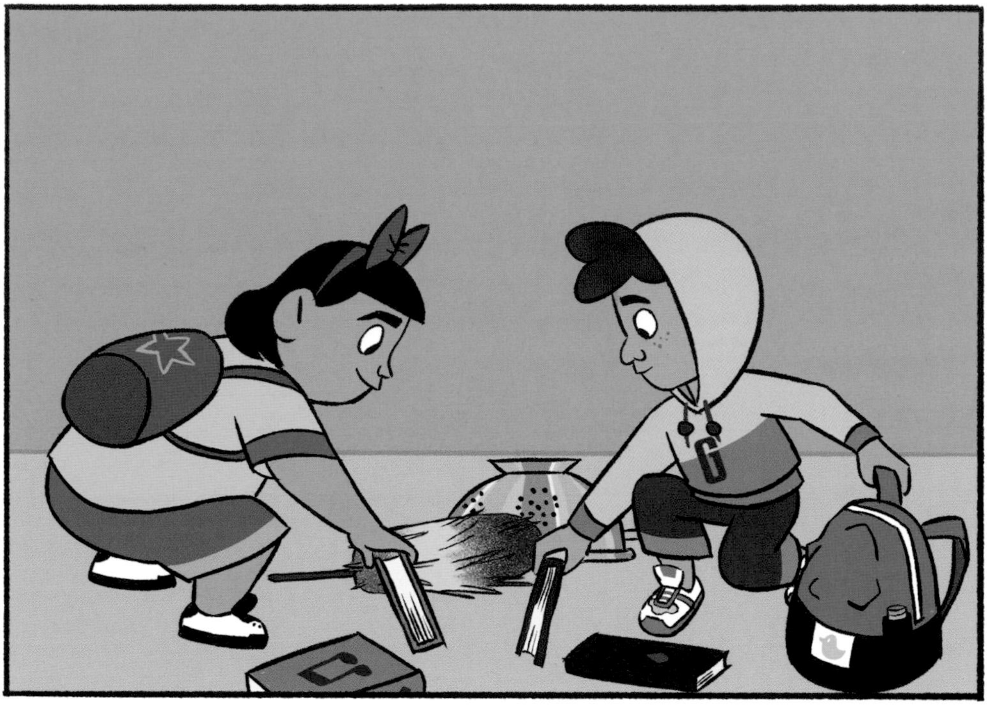

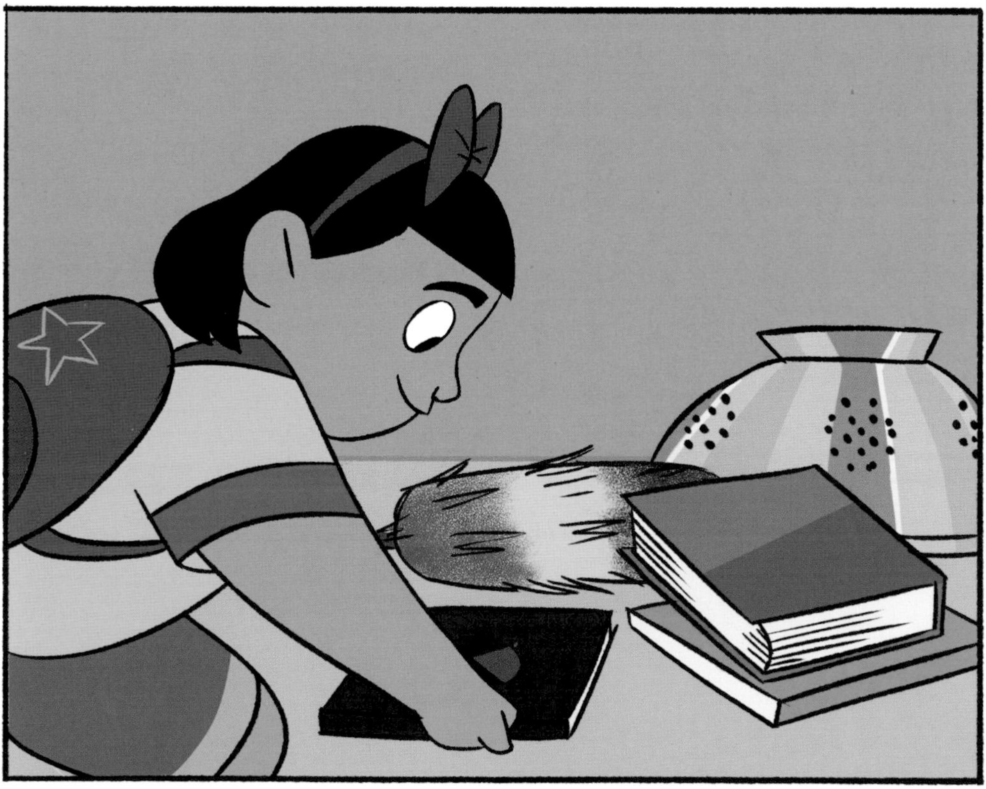

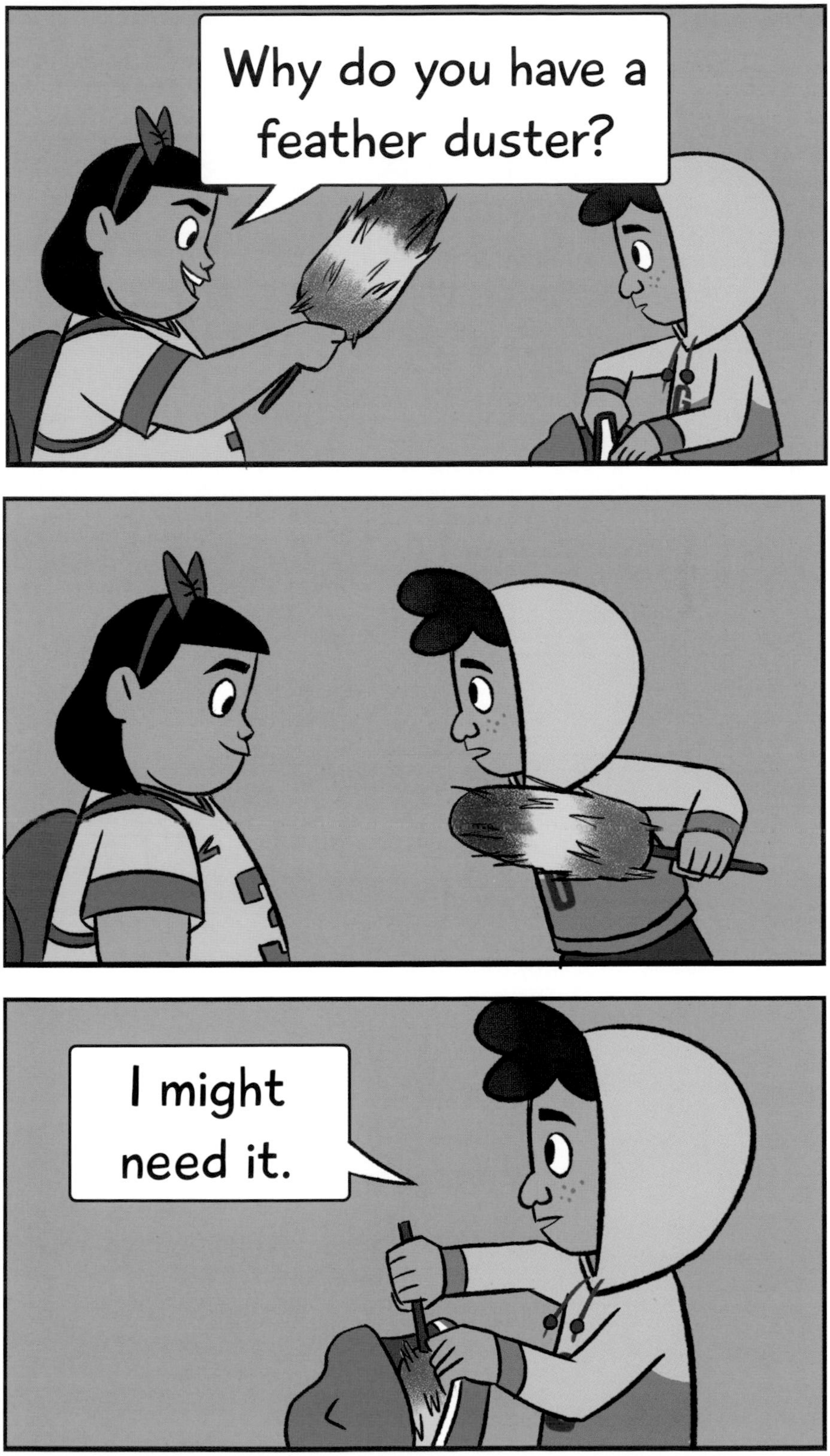
Why do you have a feather duster?
I might need it.

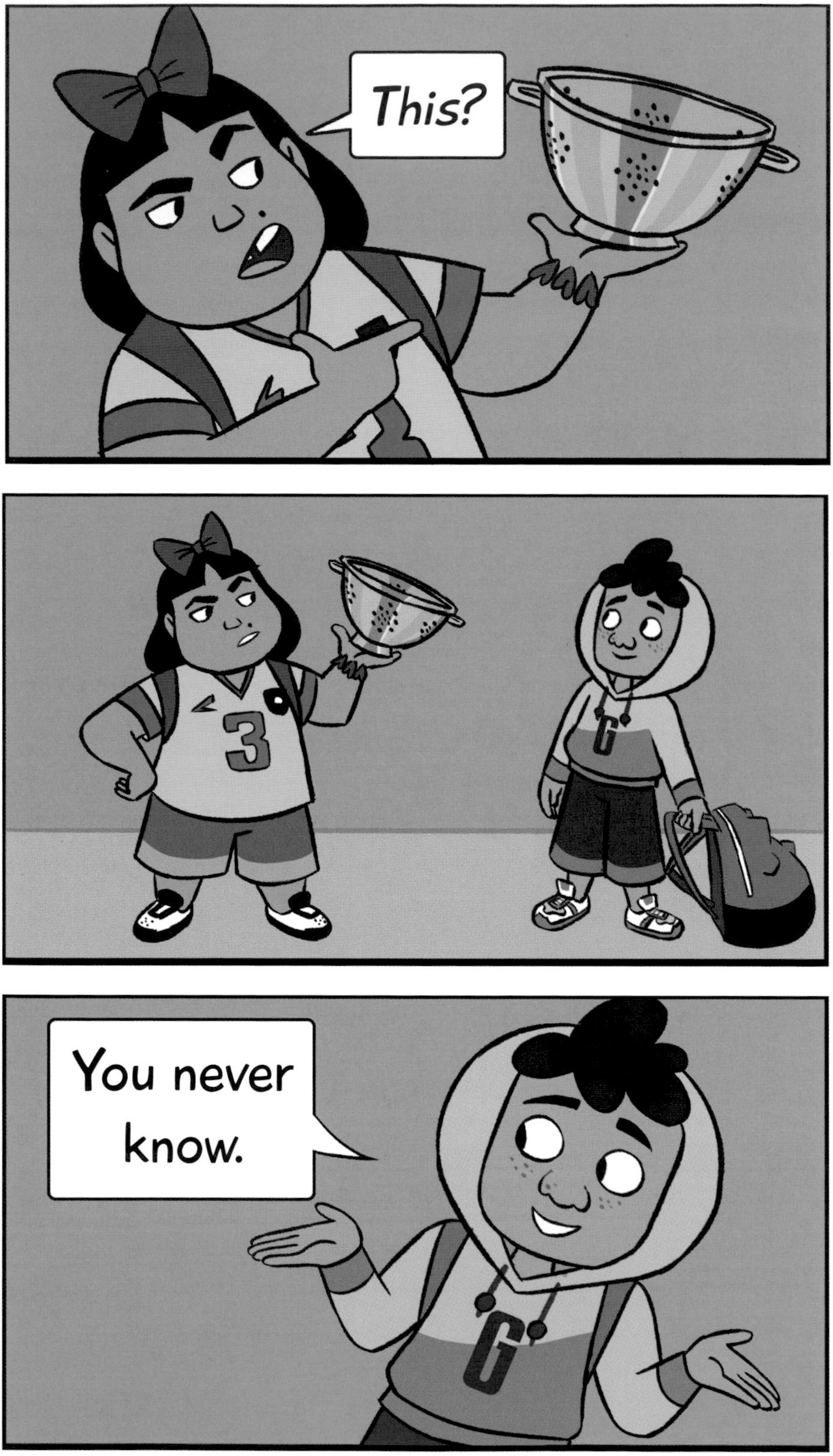
This?
You never know.

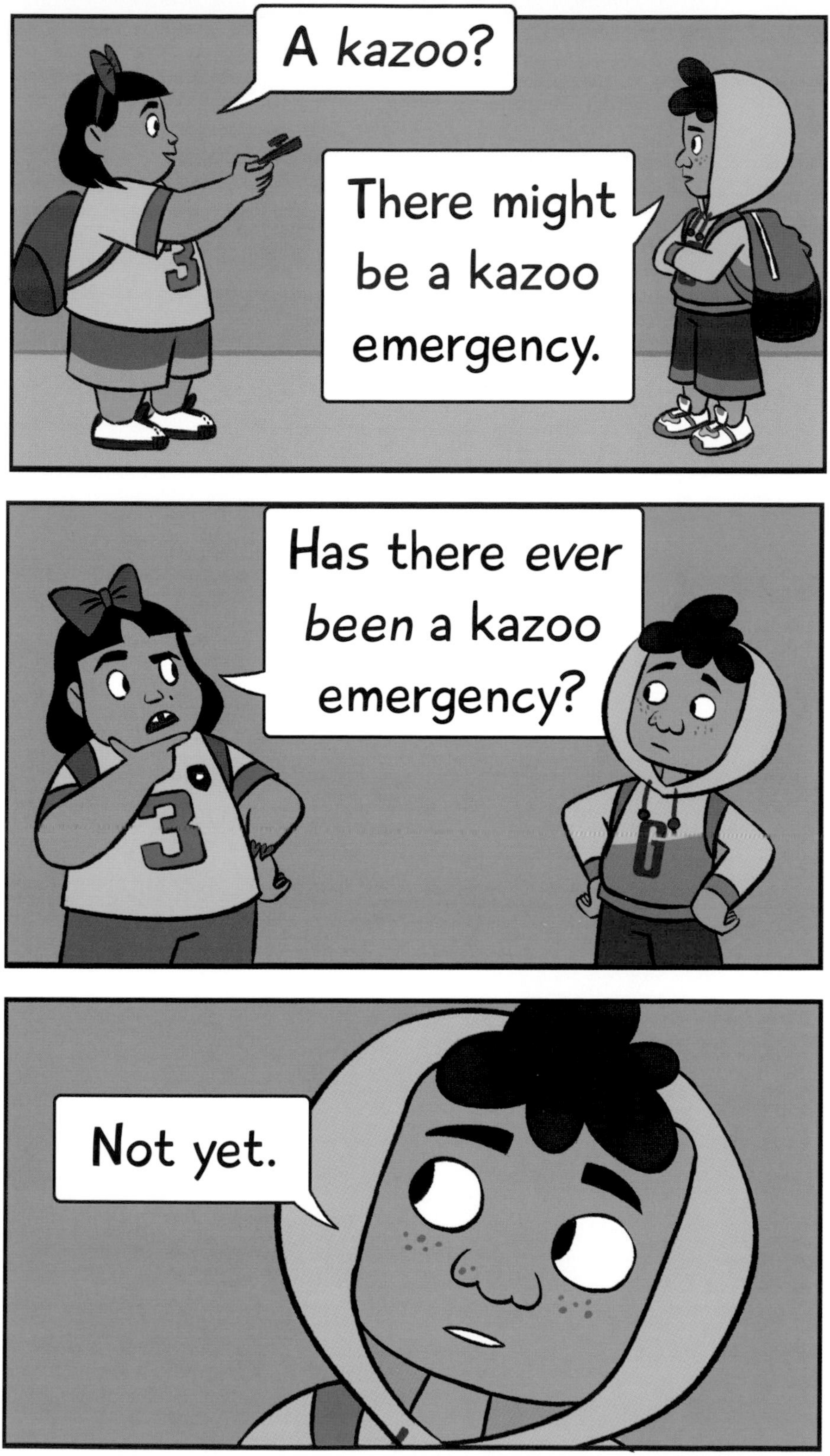
A *kazoo*?
There might be a kazoo emergency.
Has there *ever* *been* a kazoo emergency?
Not yet.

CHAPTER 3: NEW FRIENDS

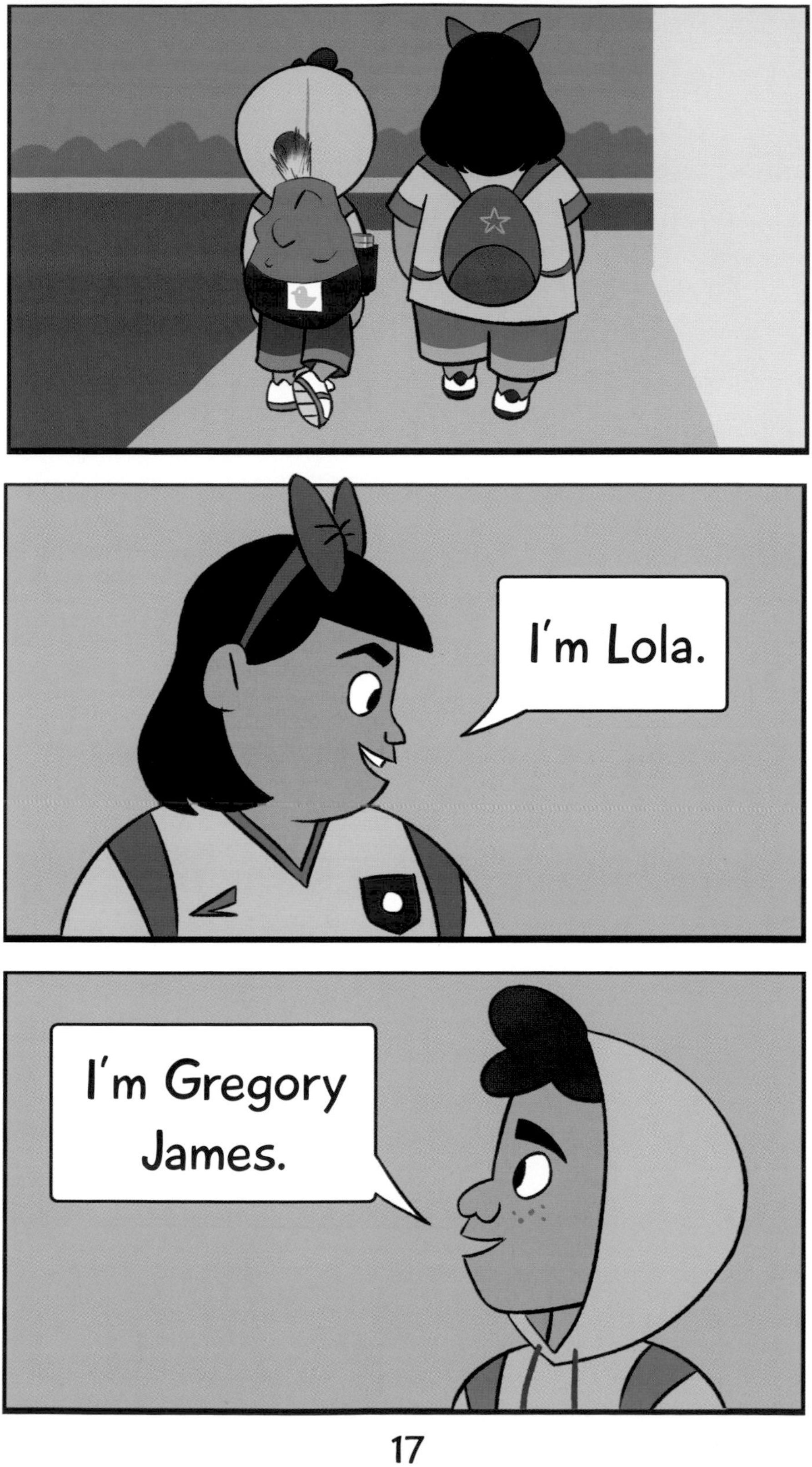

I'm Lola.
I'm Gregory James.

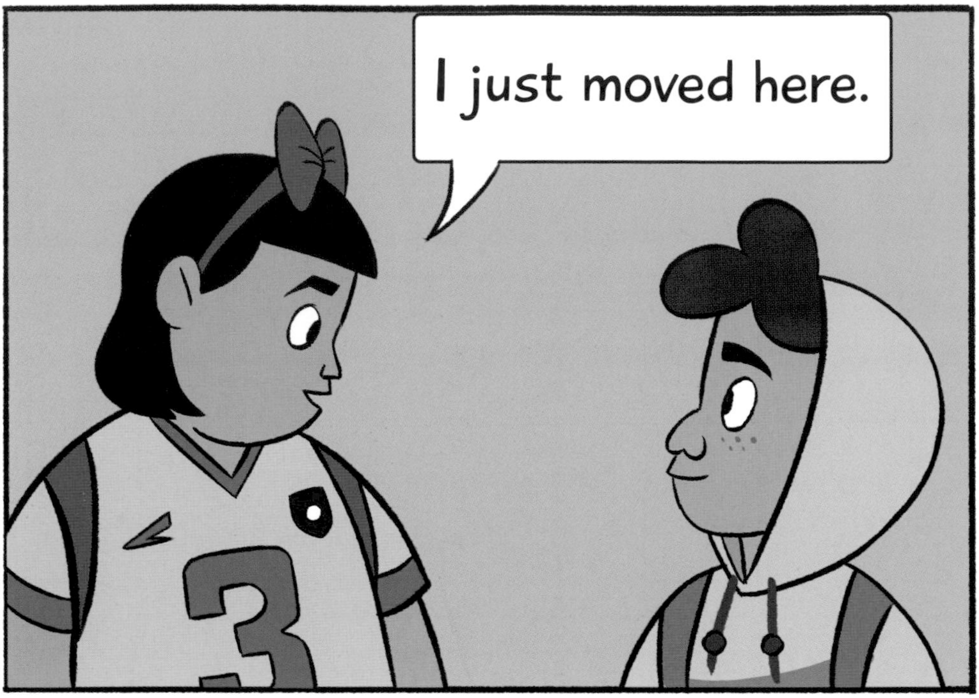
I just moved here.

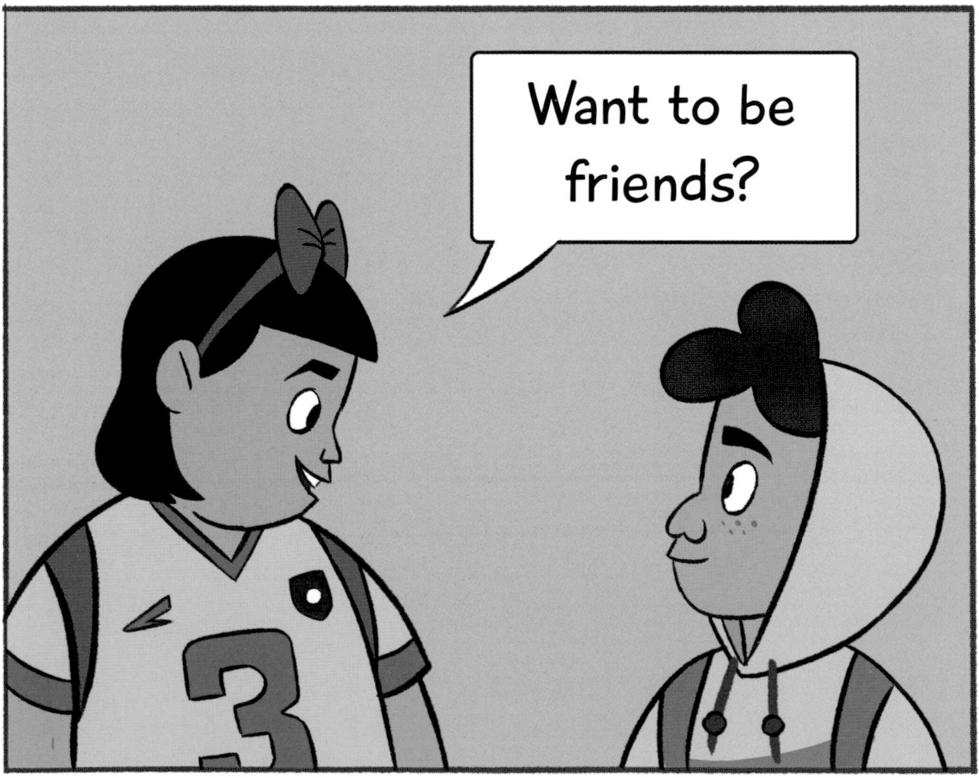
Want to be friends?

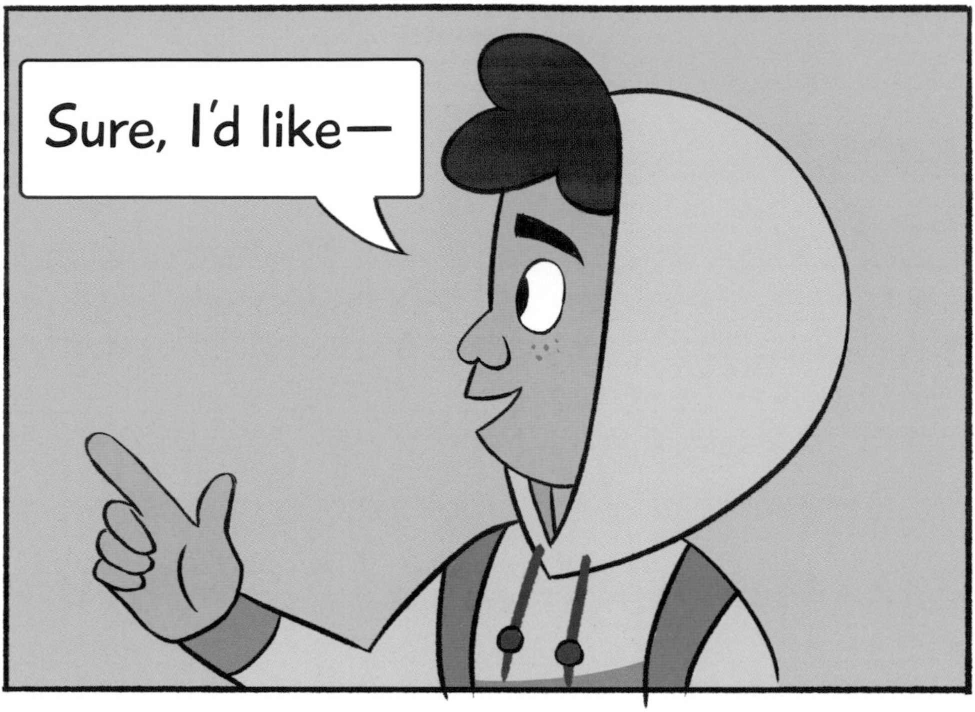
Sure, I'd like—

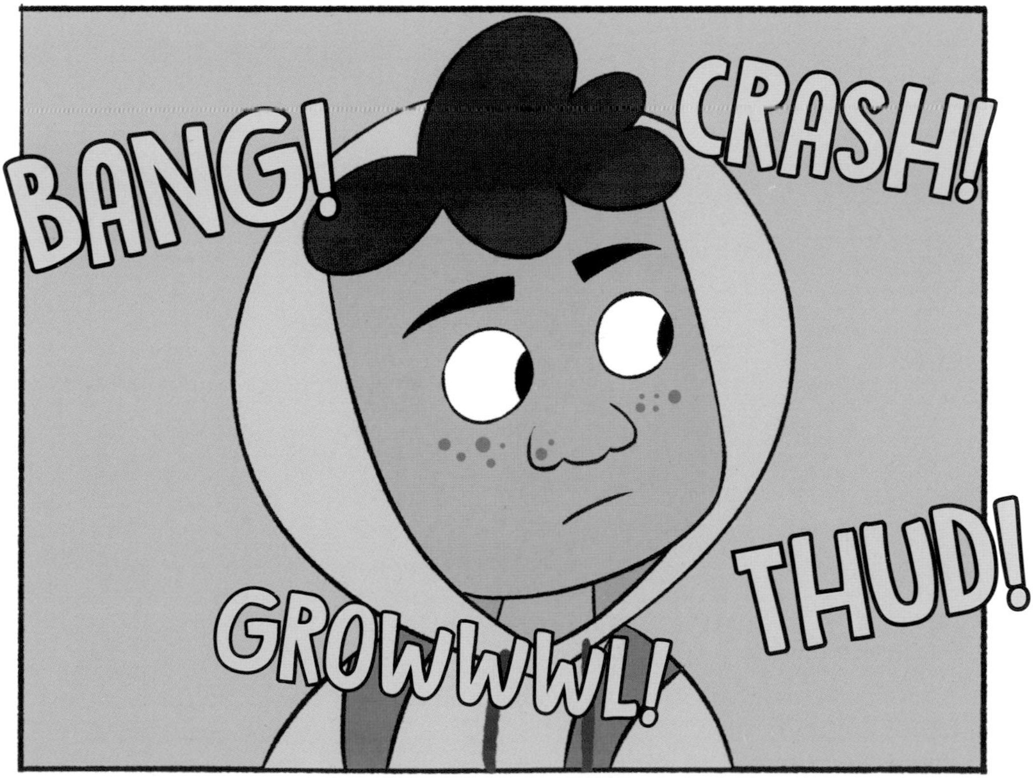
BANG!
CRASH!
GROWWWL!
THUD!

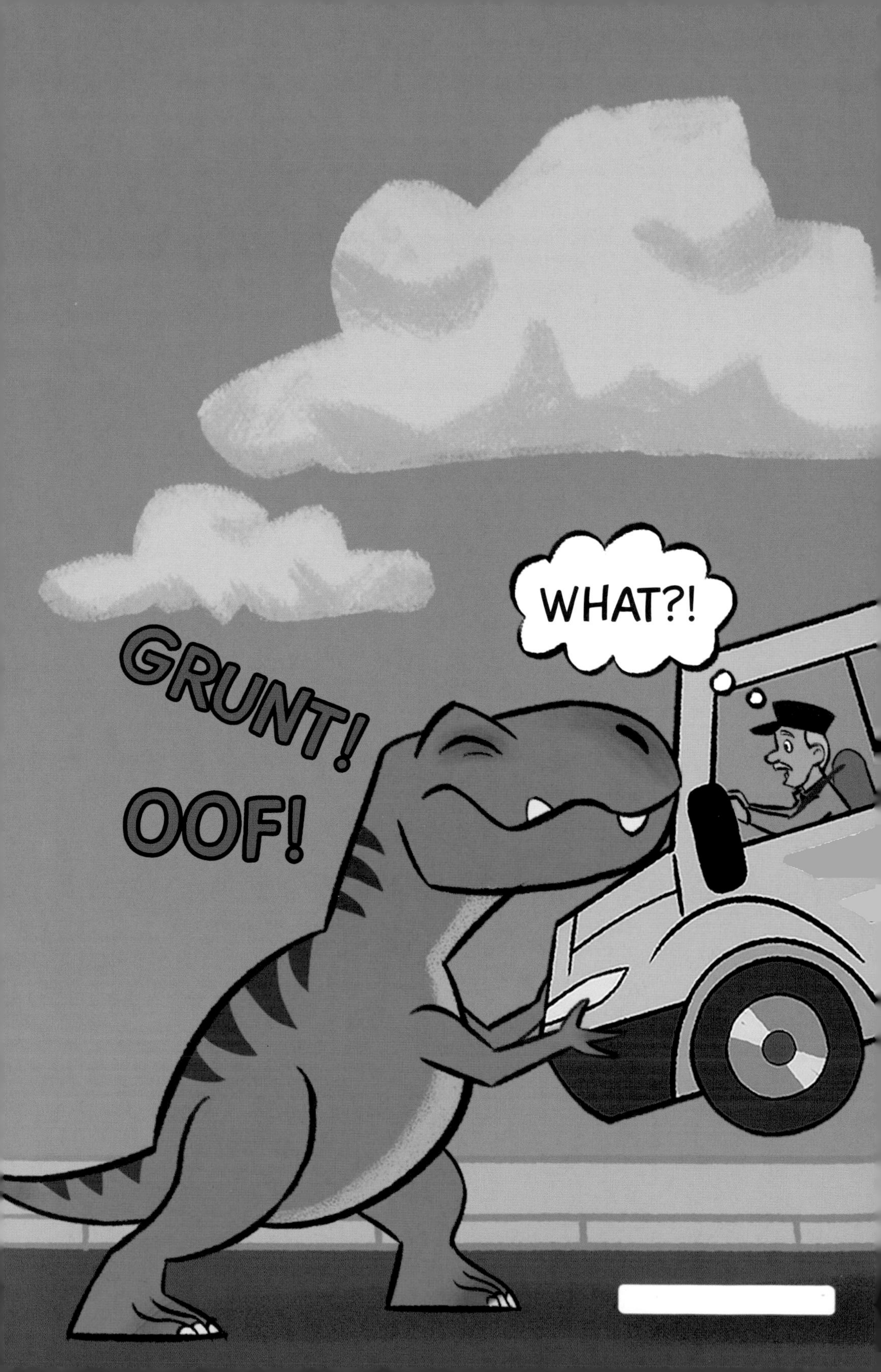
GRUNT!
OOF!
WHAT?!

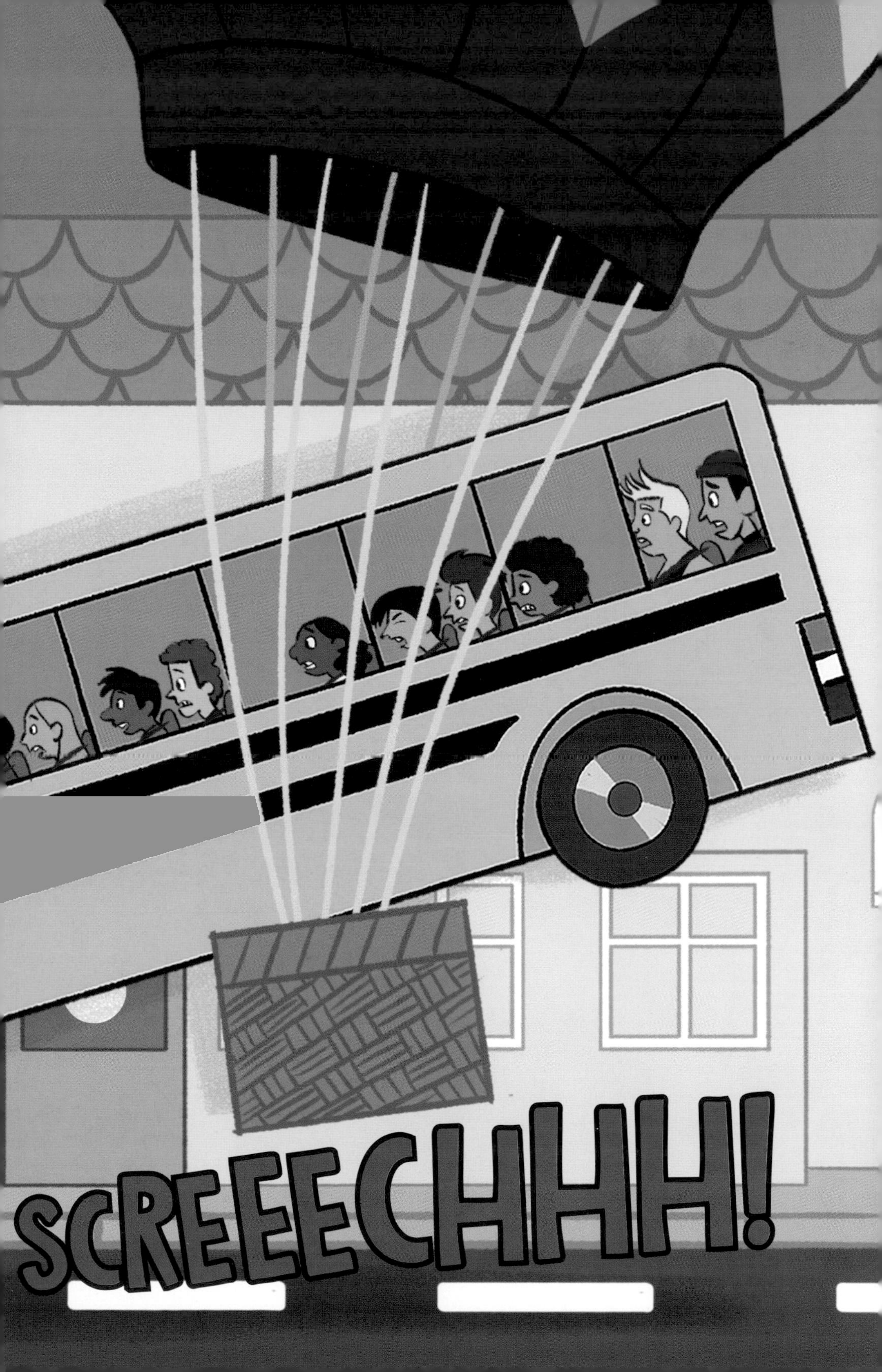
SCREEECHHH!

CHAPTER 4: AN UNEXPECTED SITUATION

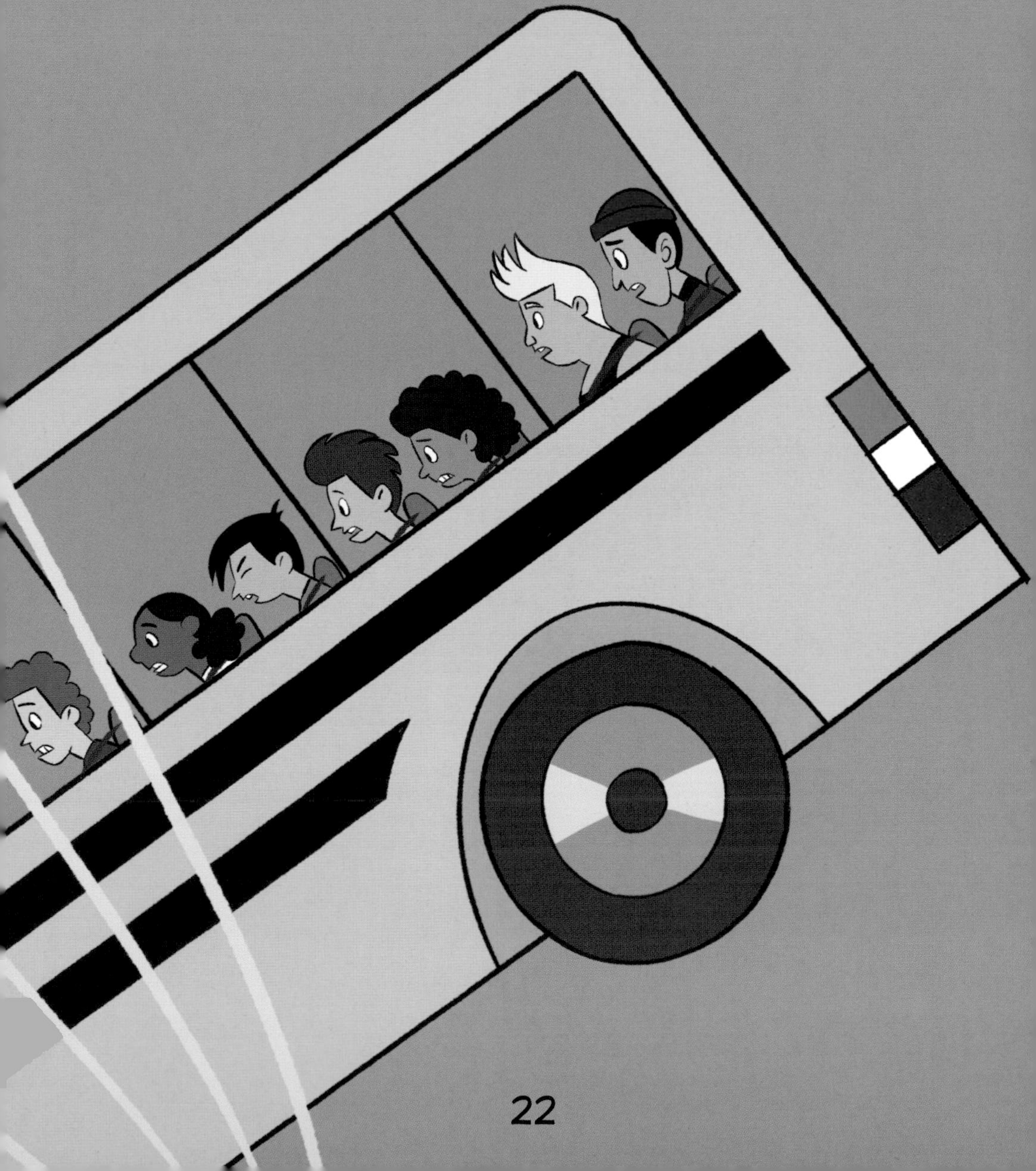

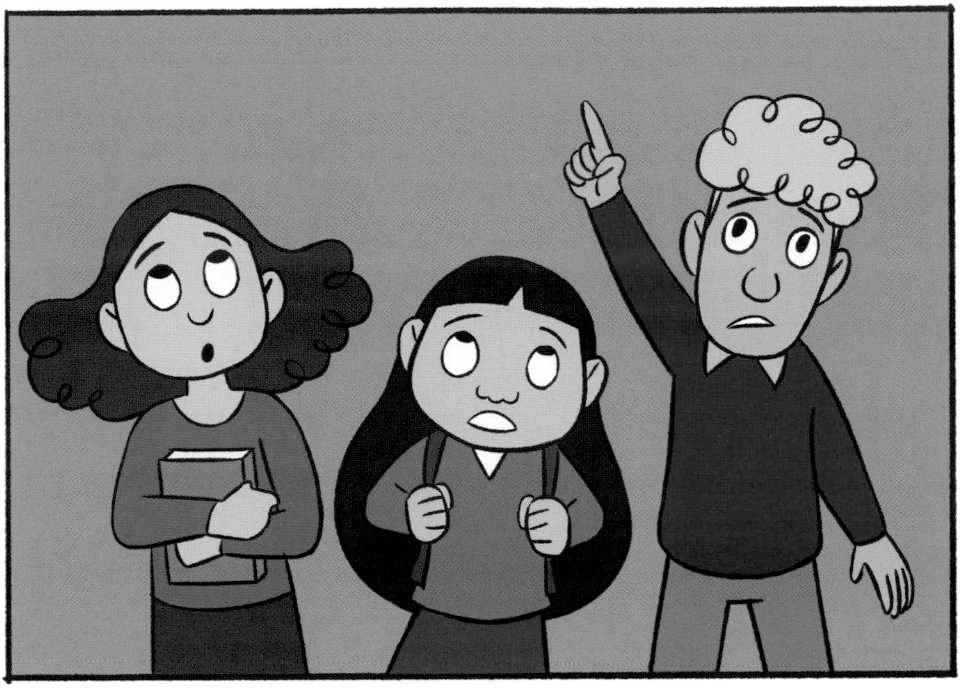

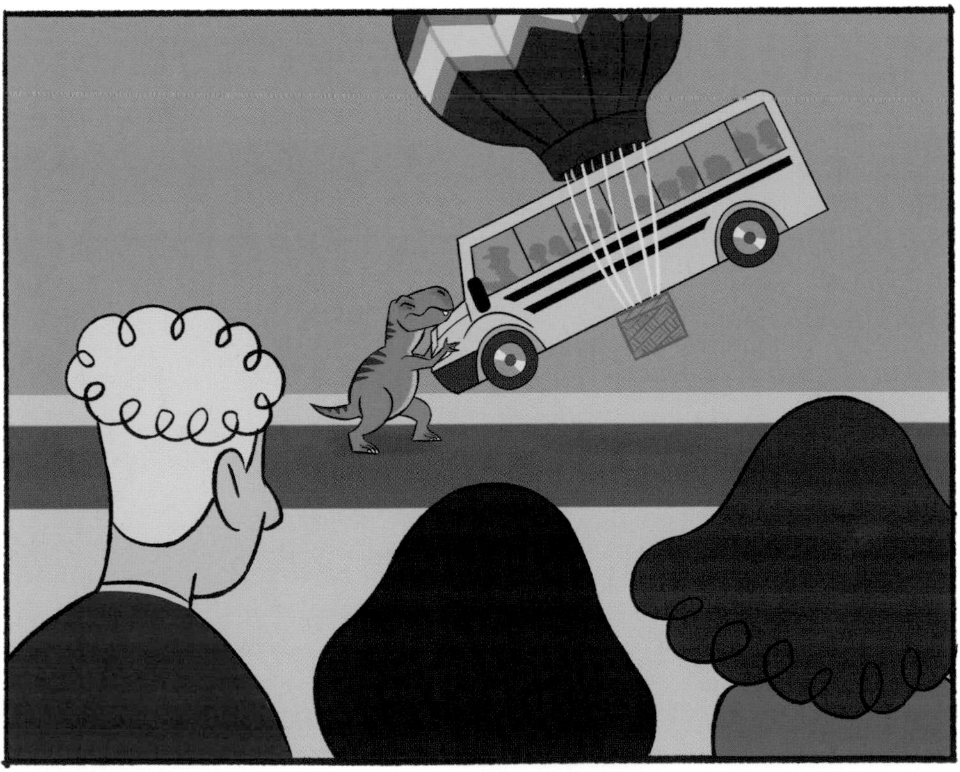

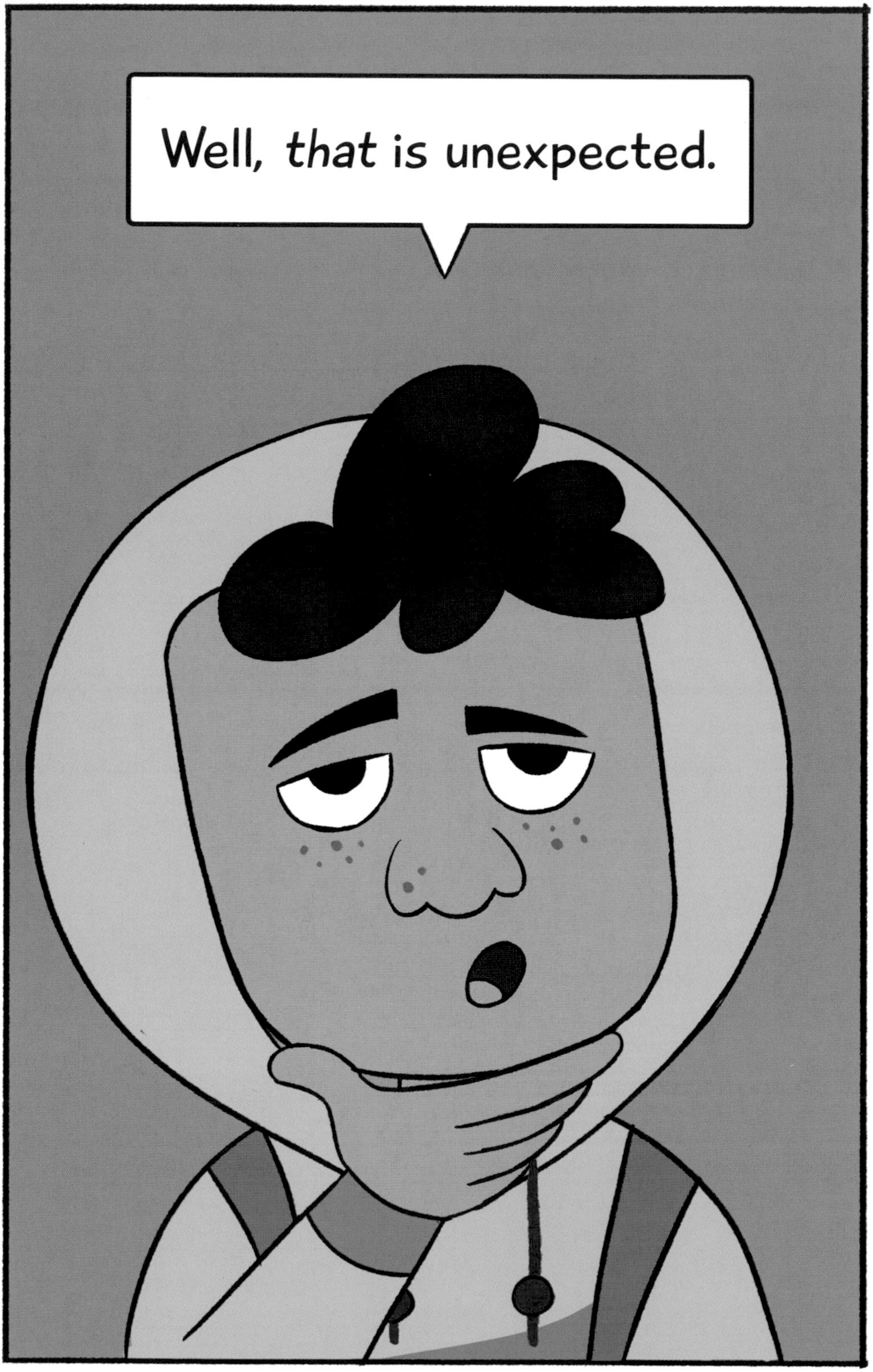
Well, *that* is unexpected.

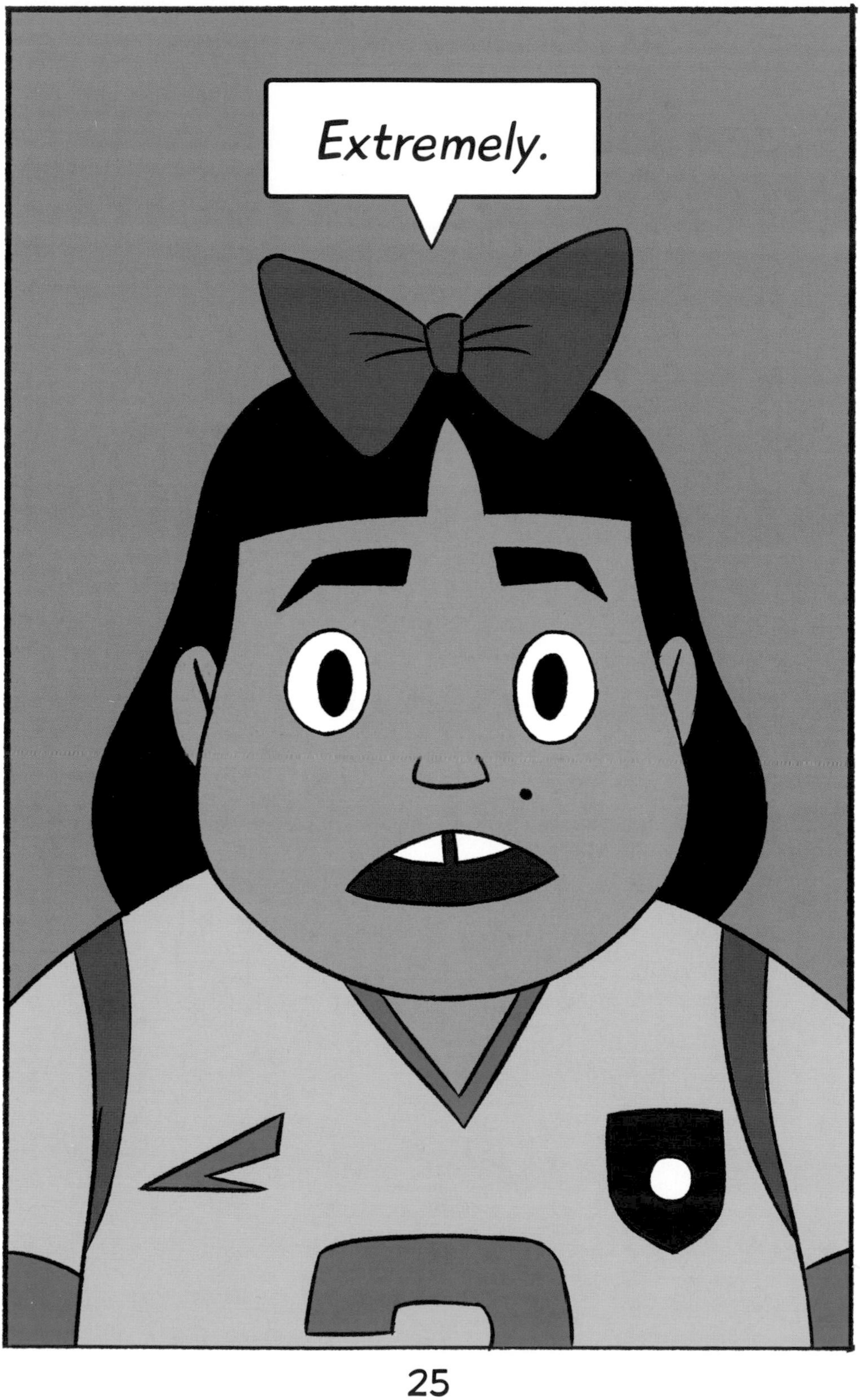
Extremely.

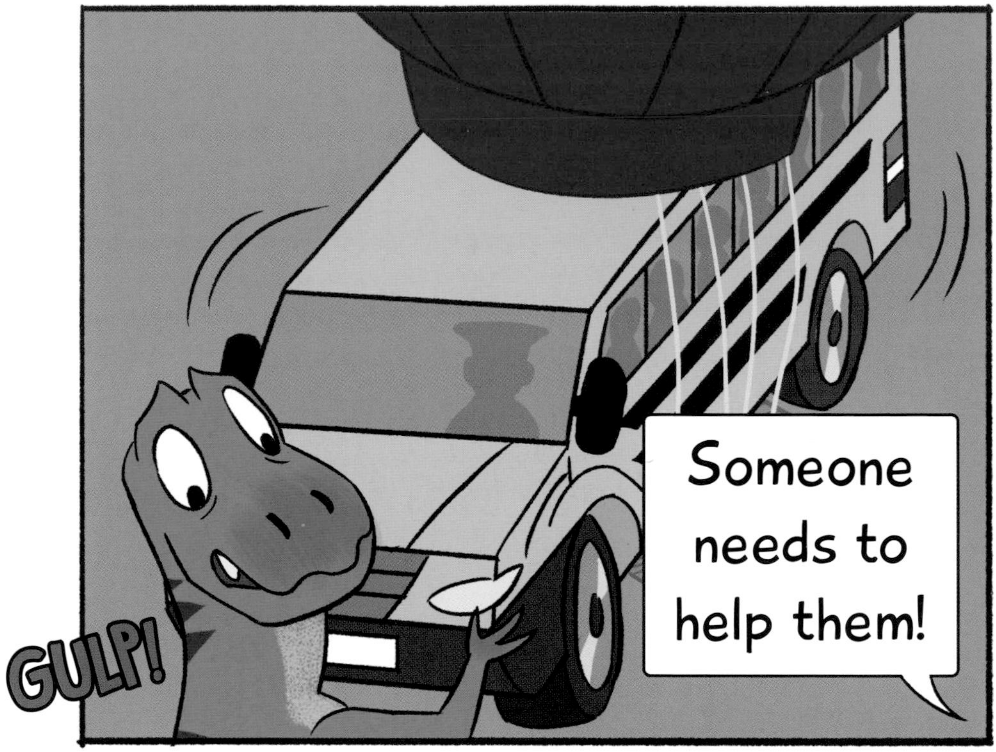
Someone needs to help them!
GULP!

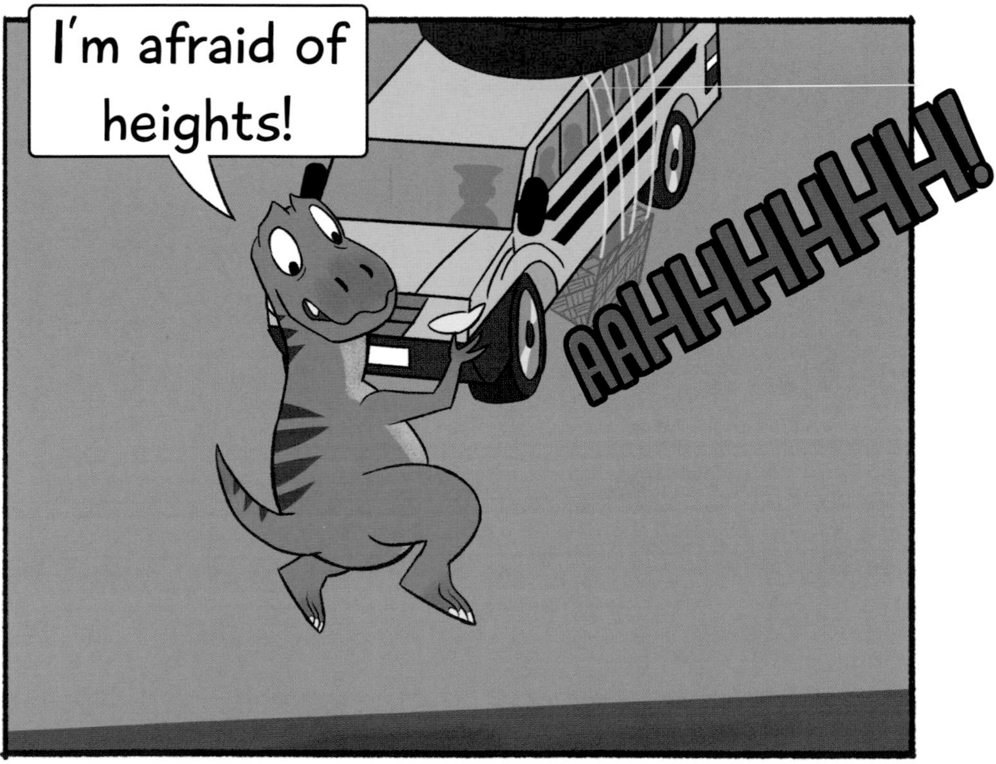
I'm afraid of heights!
AAHHHHHHH!

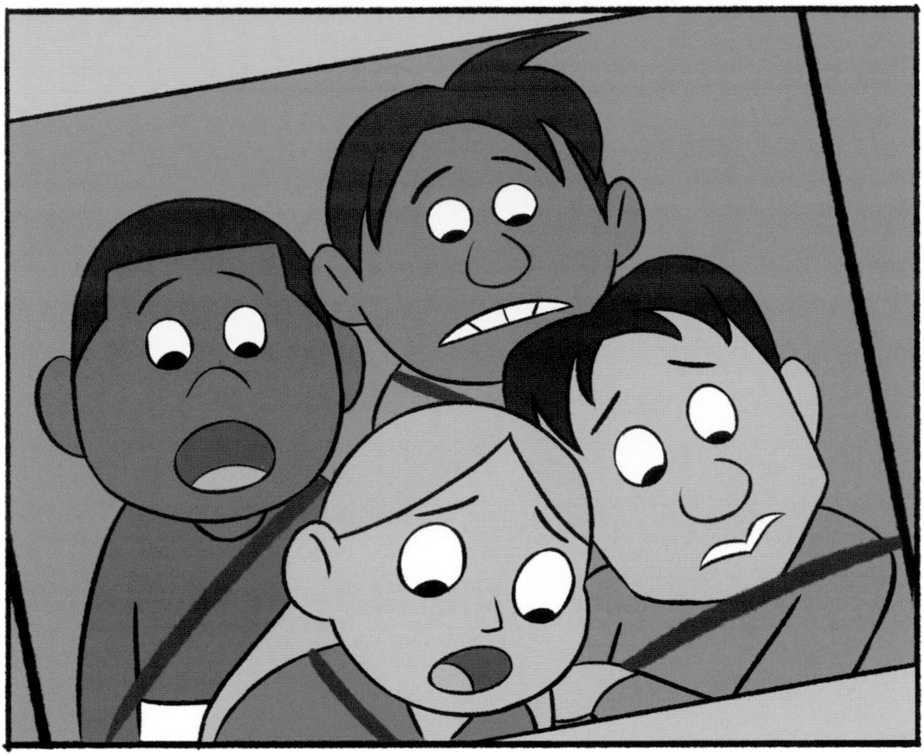

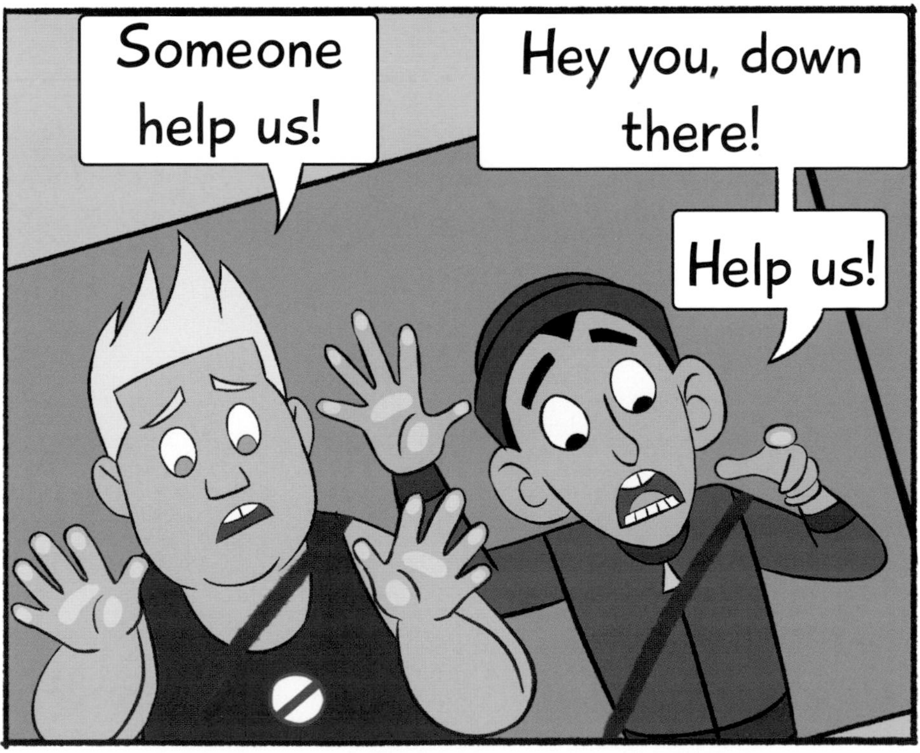
Someone help us!
Hey you, down there!
Help us!

CHAPTER 5: TICKLISH

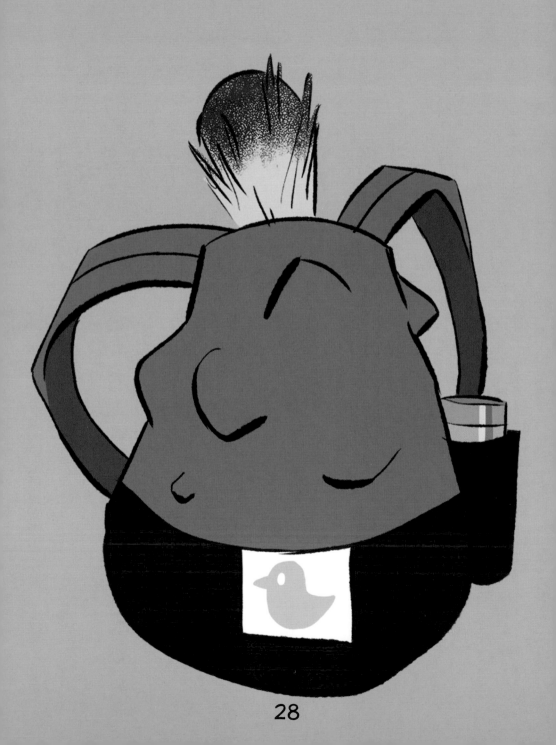

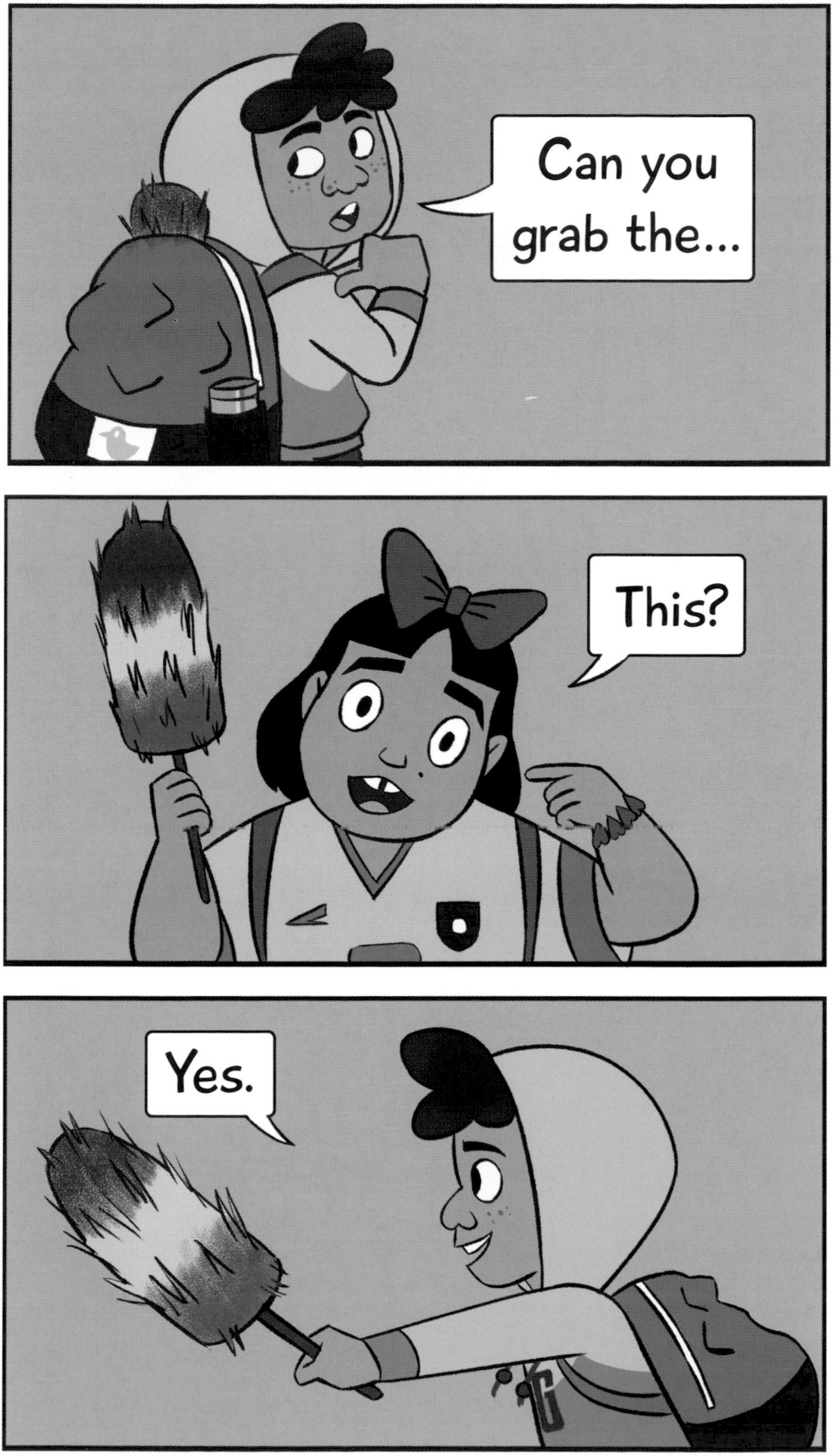

Can you grab the...
This?
Yes.

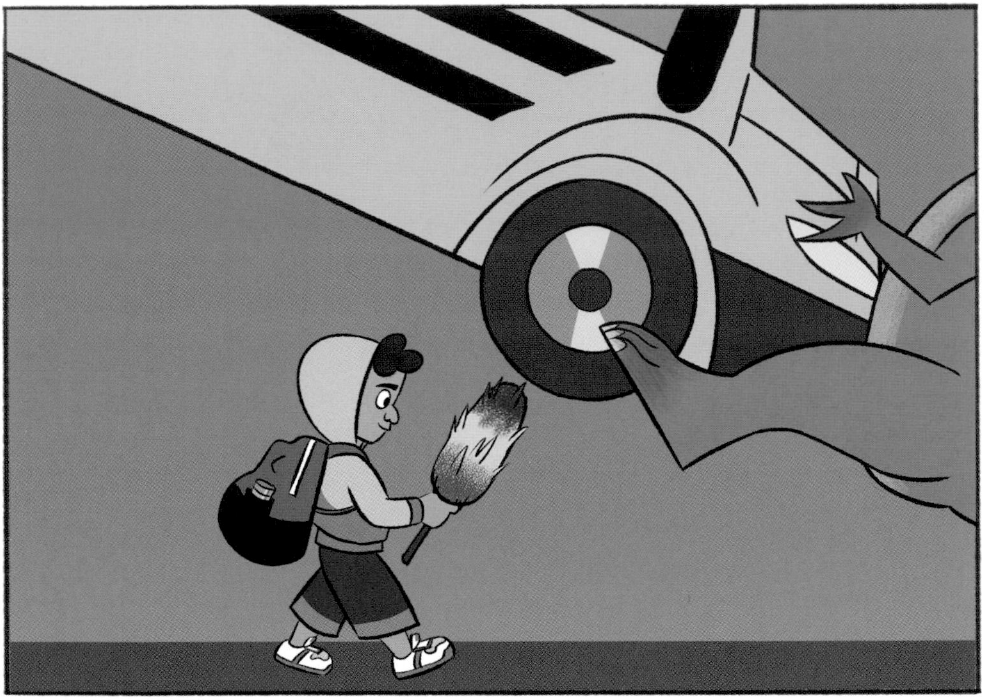

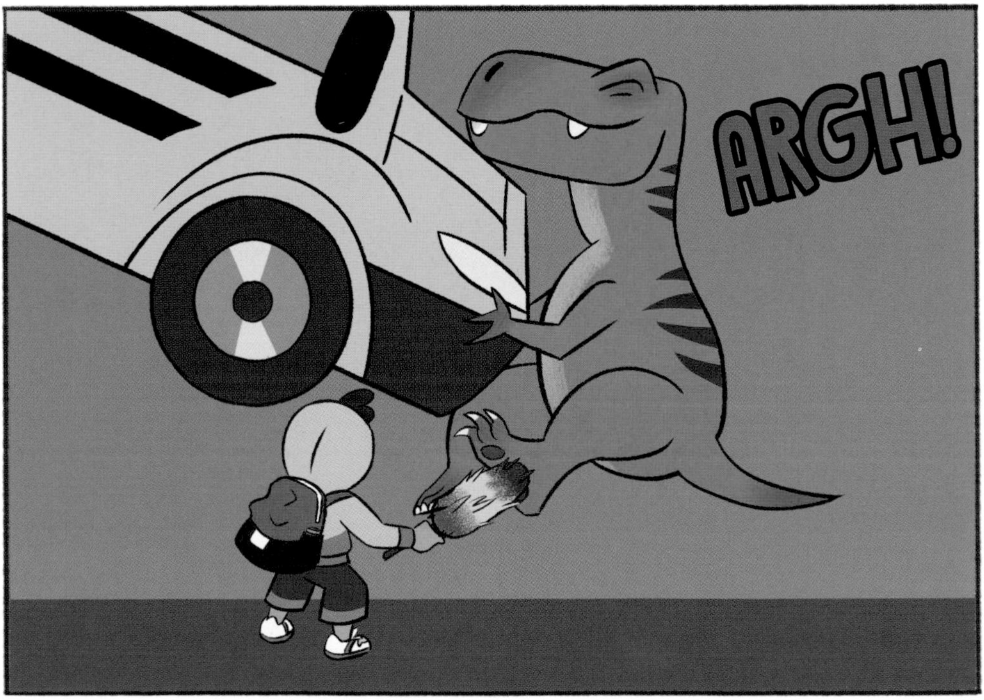
ARGH!

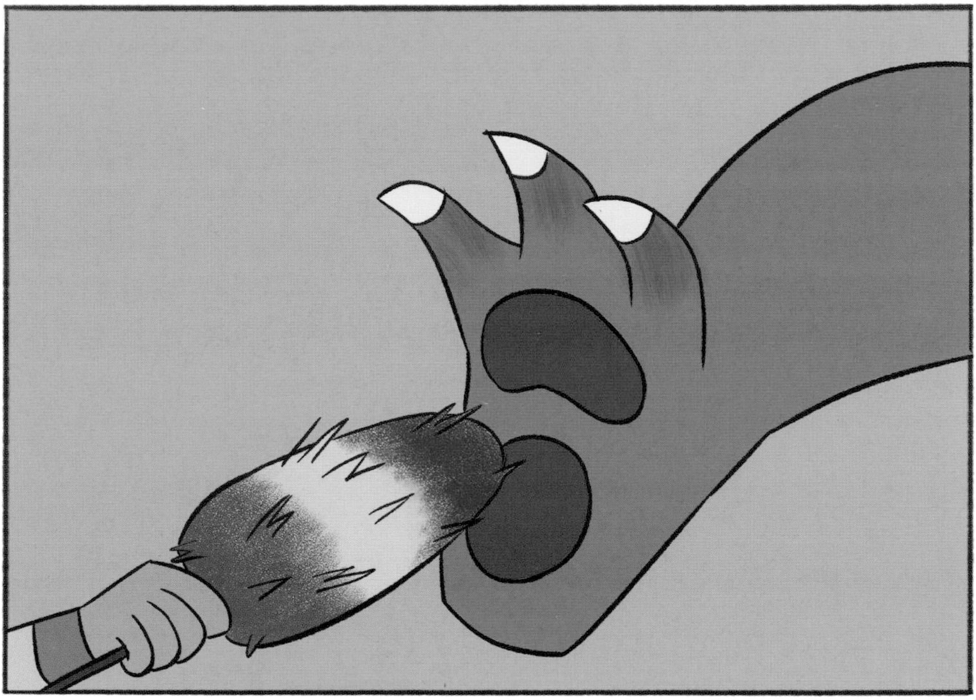

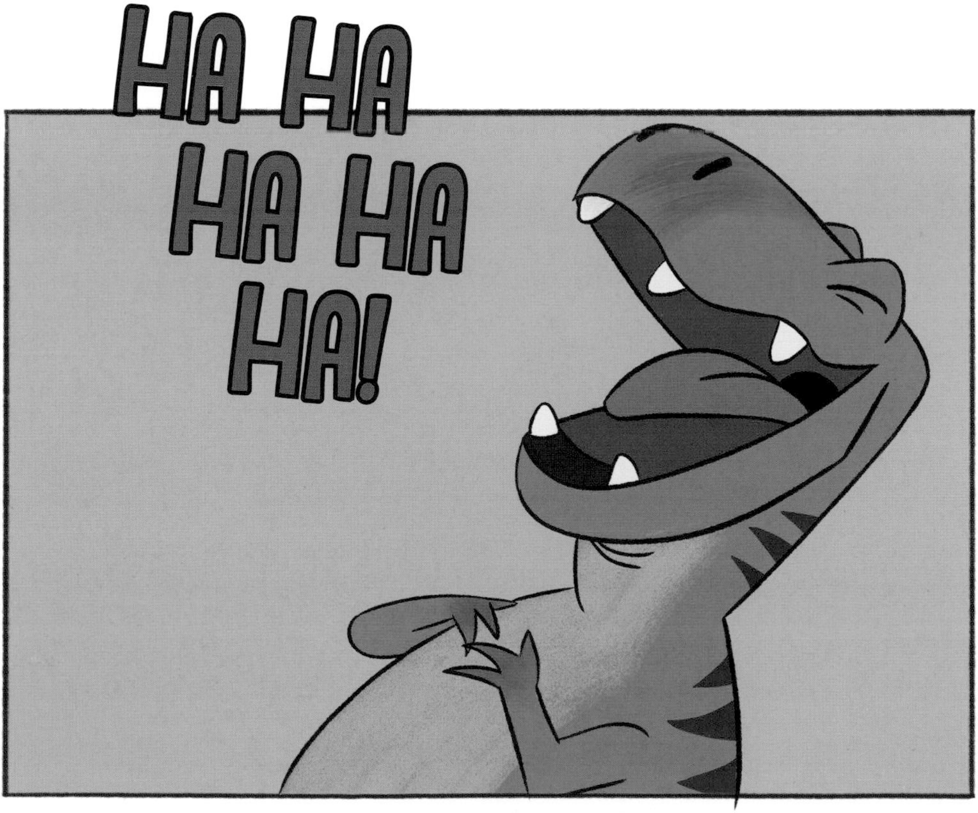
HA HA
HA HA
HA!

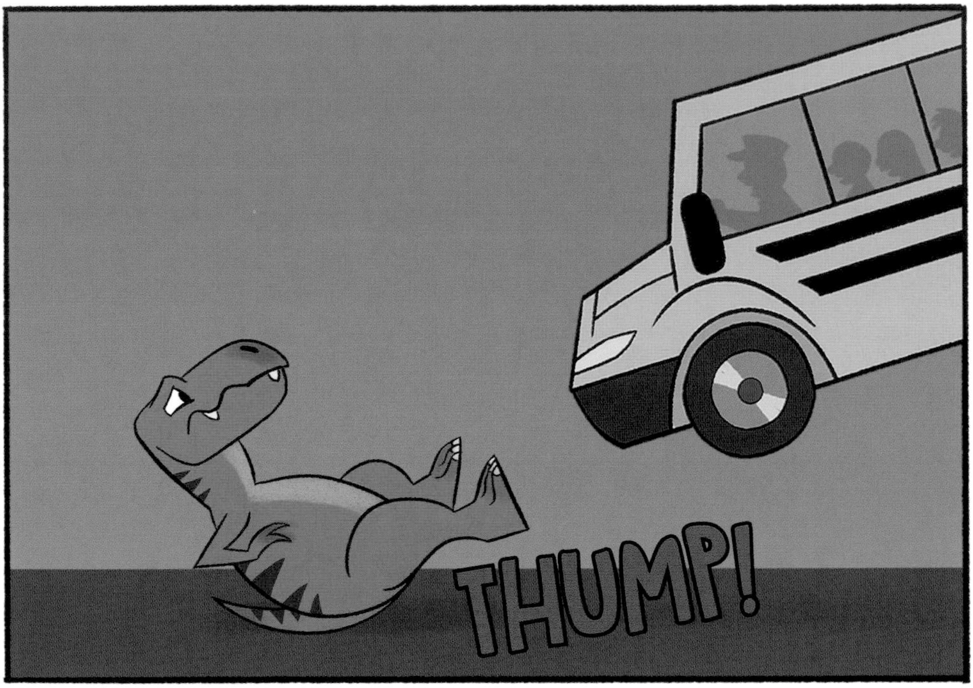
THUMP!

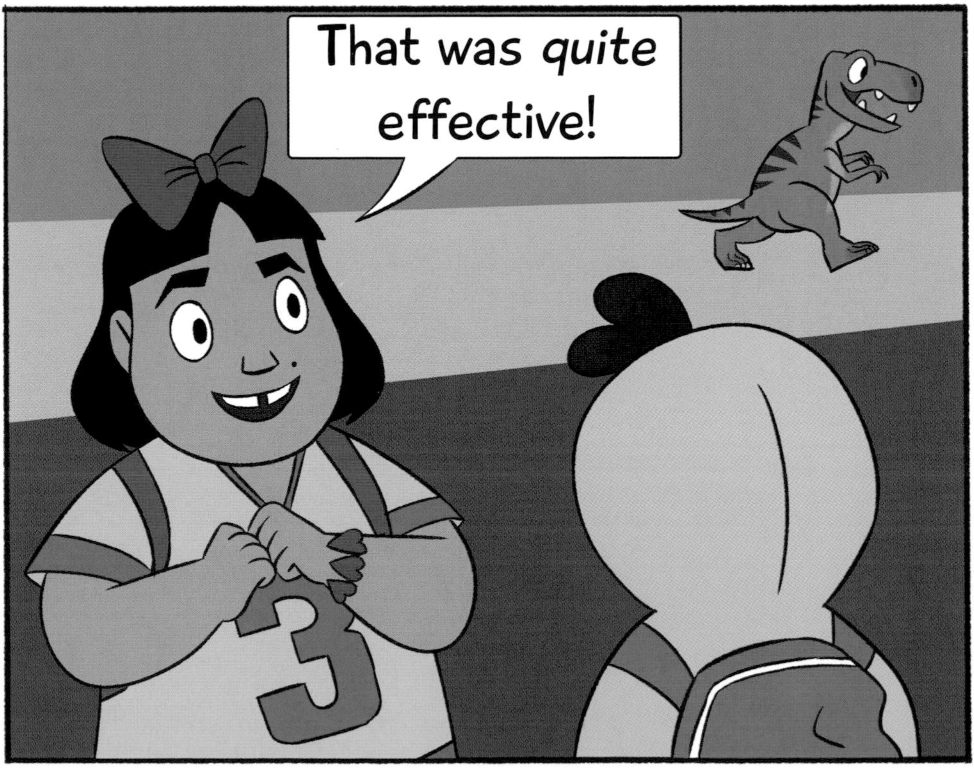
That was *quite* effective!

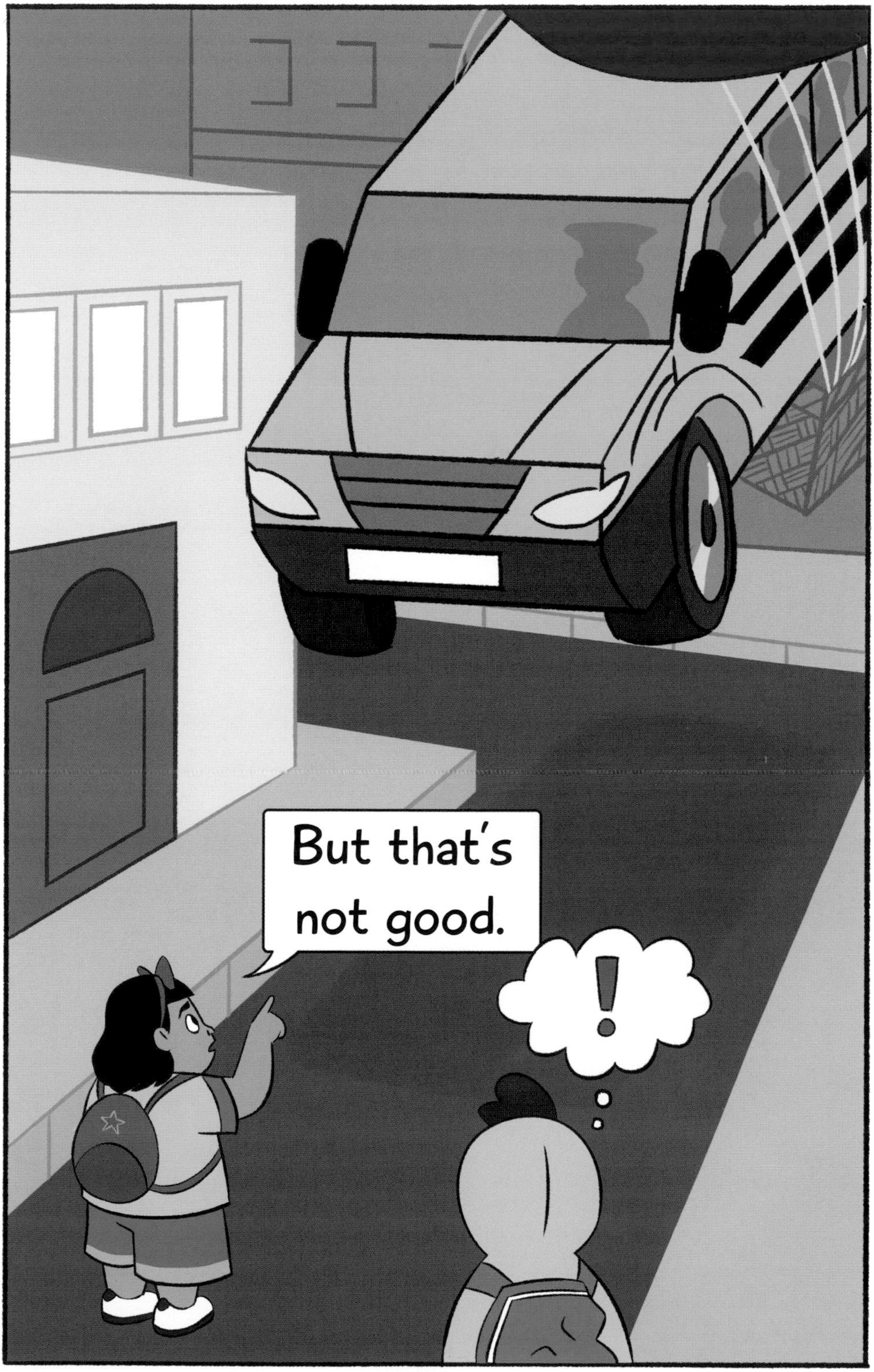
But that's not good.
!

CHAPTER 6: NOT GOOD

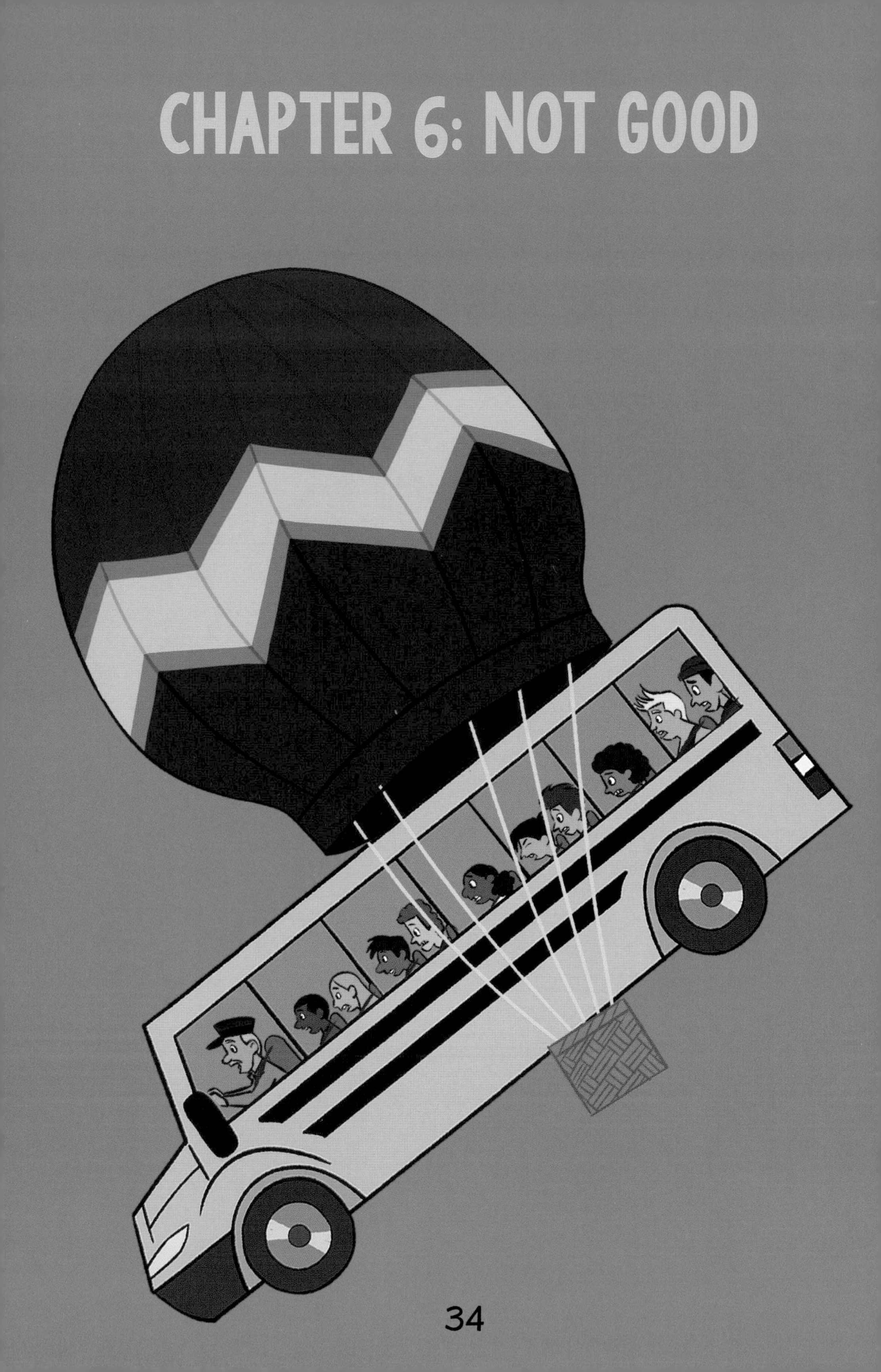

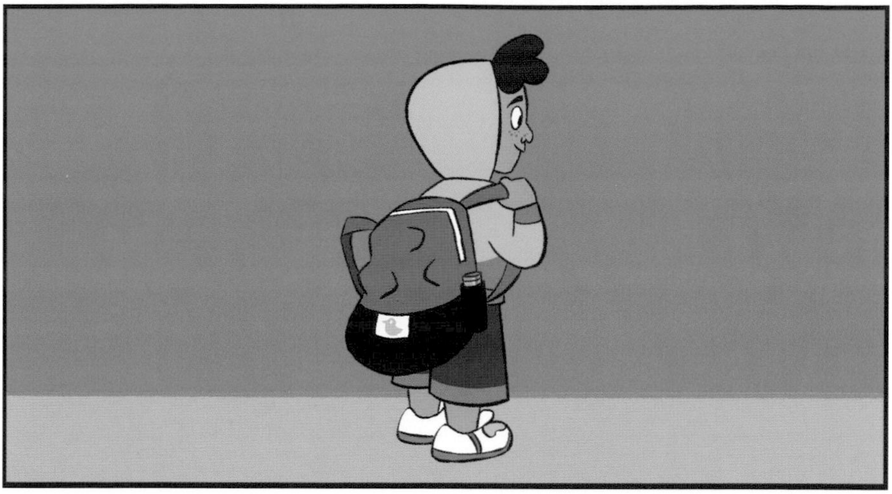

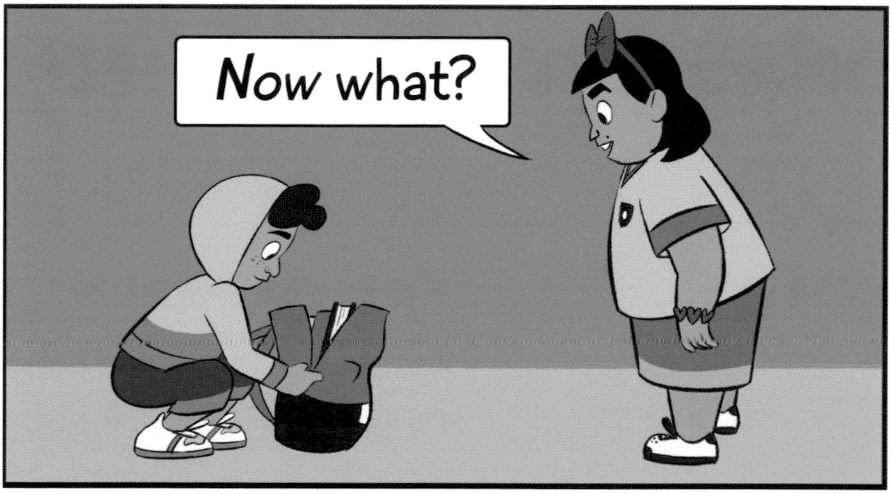
Now what?

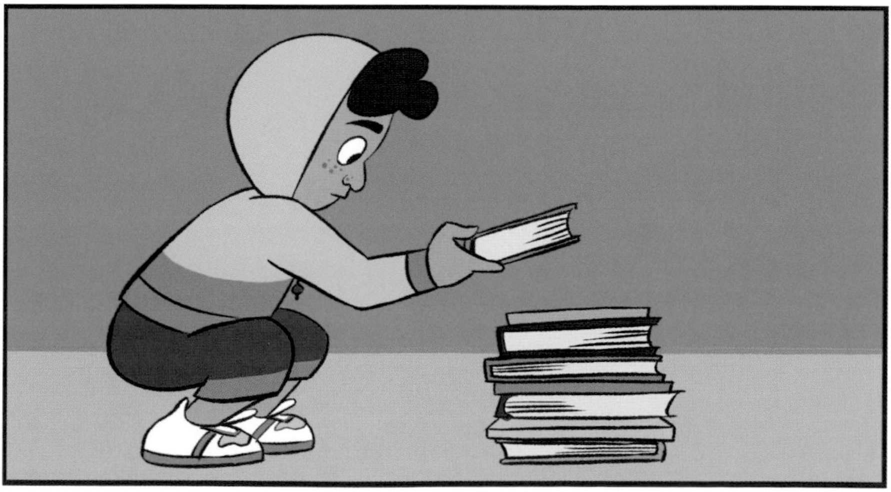

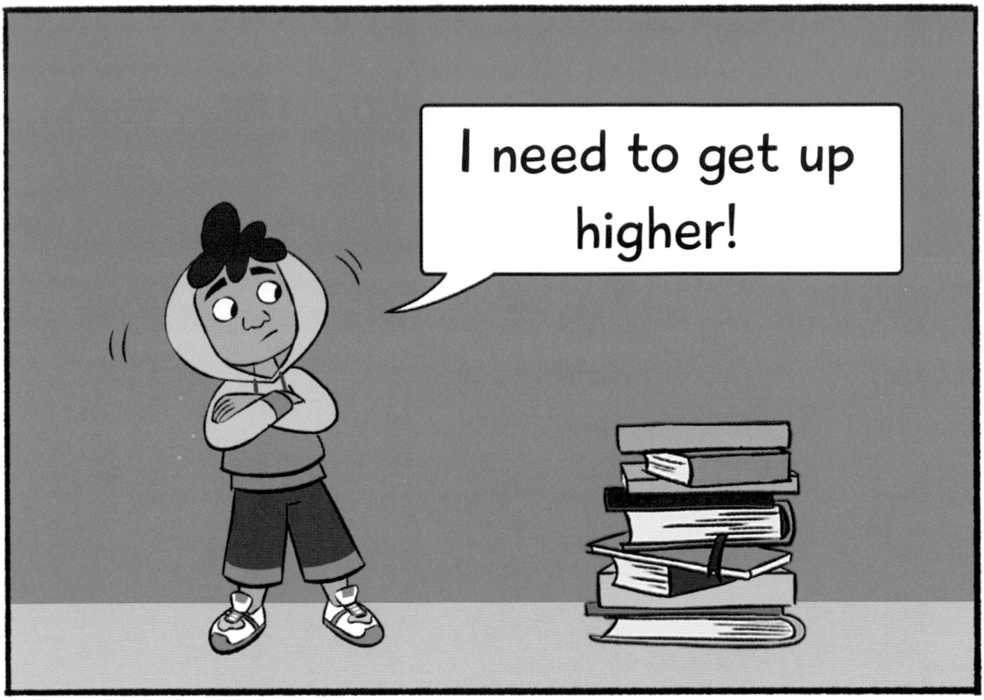
I need to get up higher!

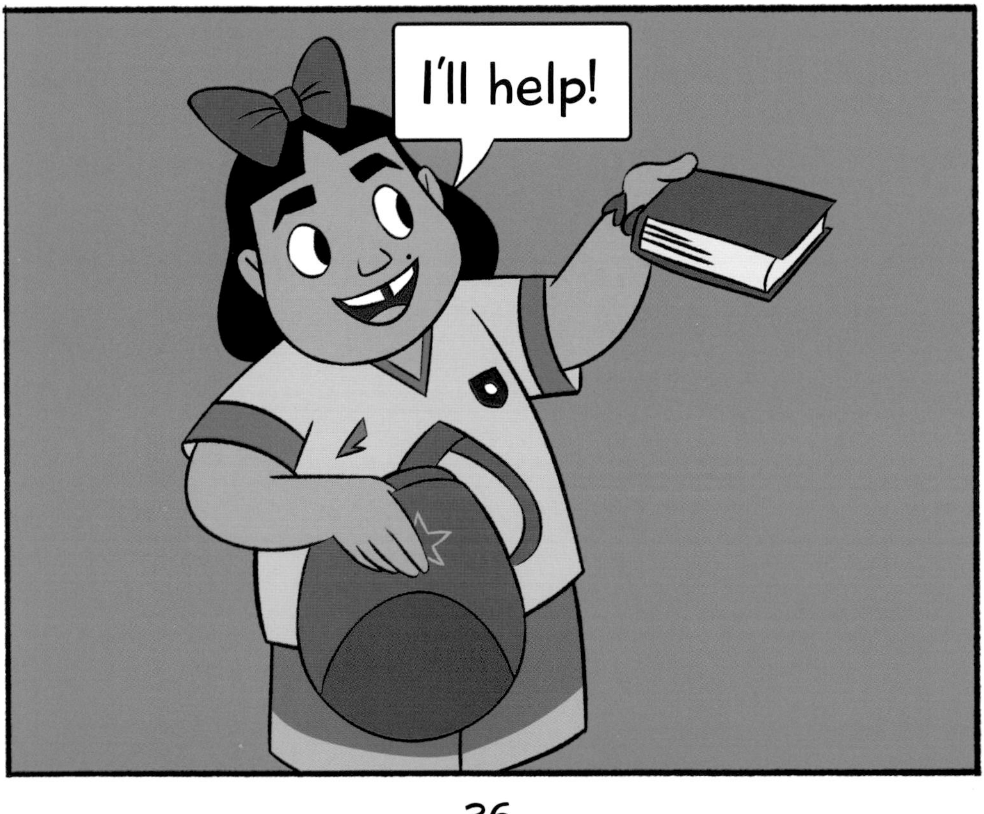
I'll help!

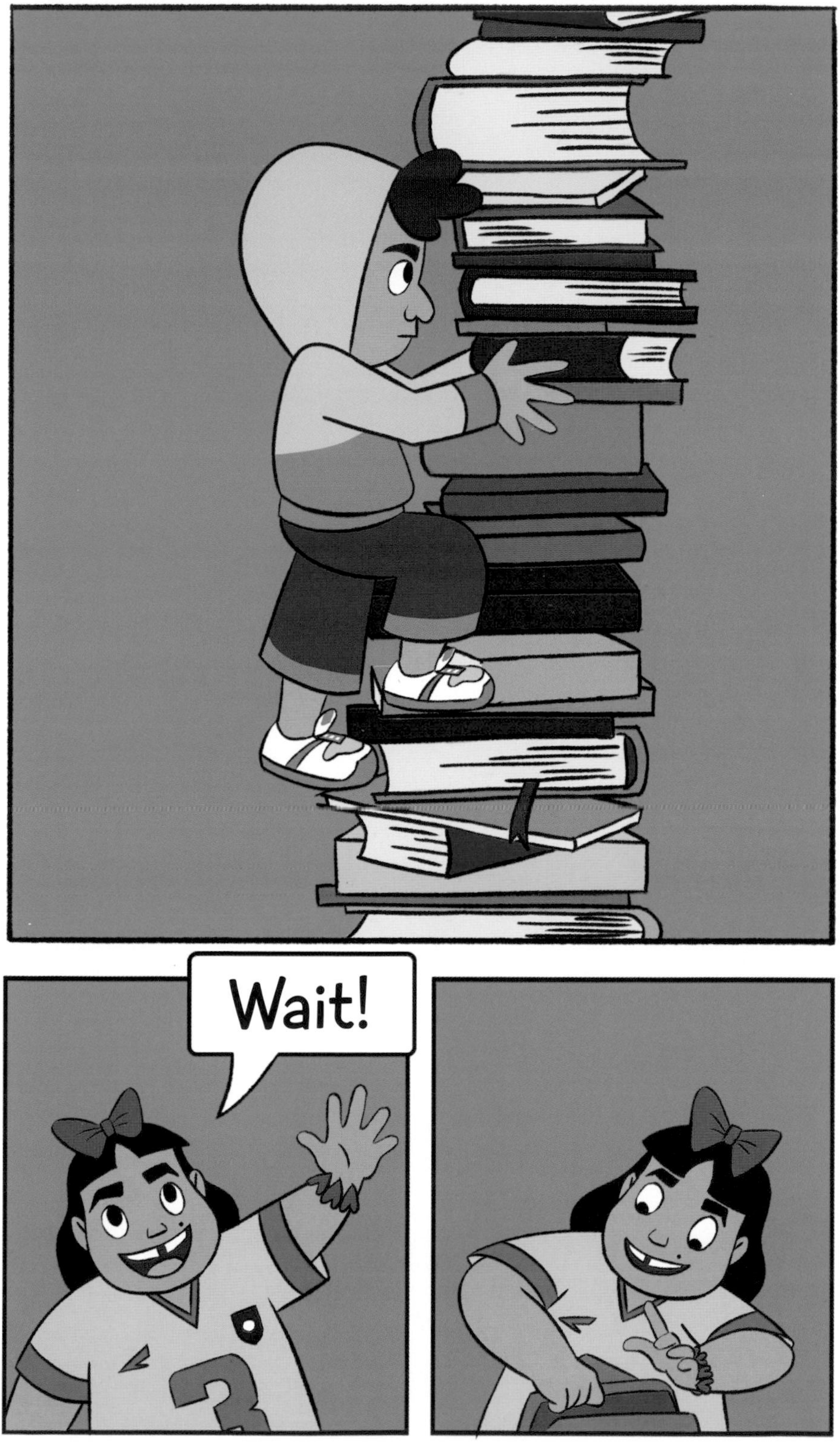
Wait!

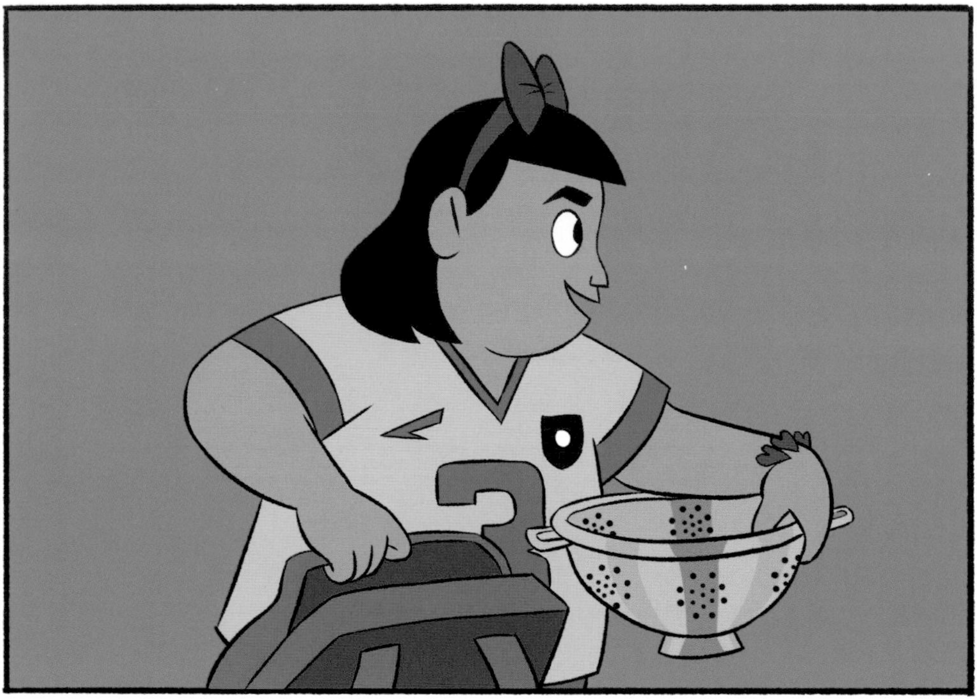

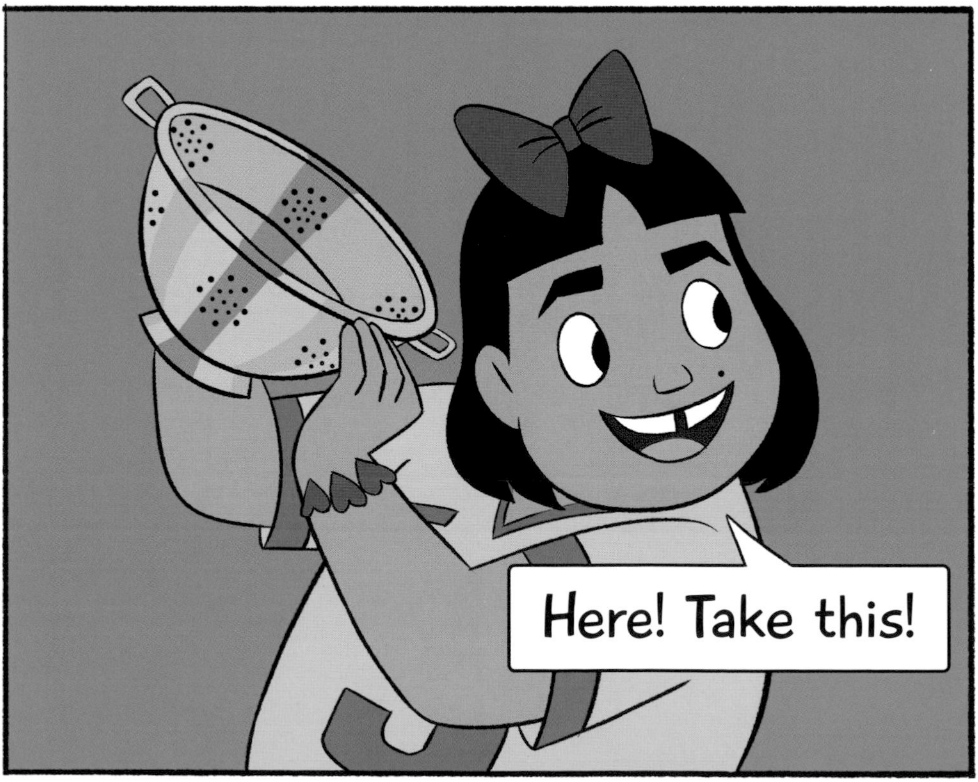
Here! Take this!

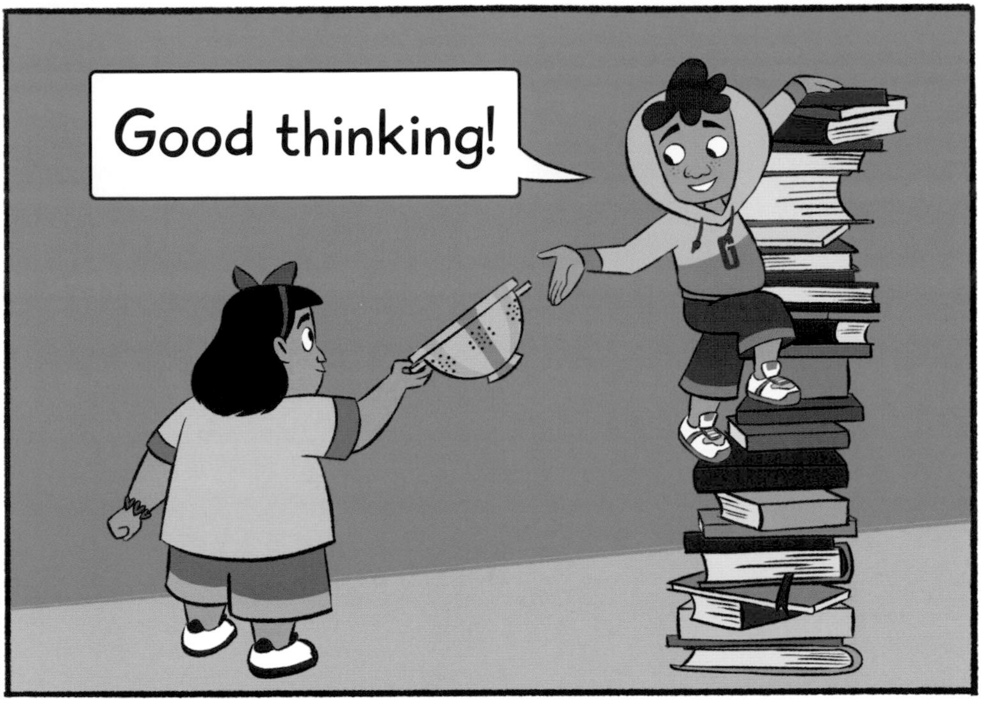
Good thinking!

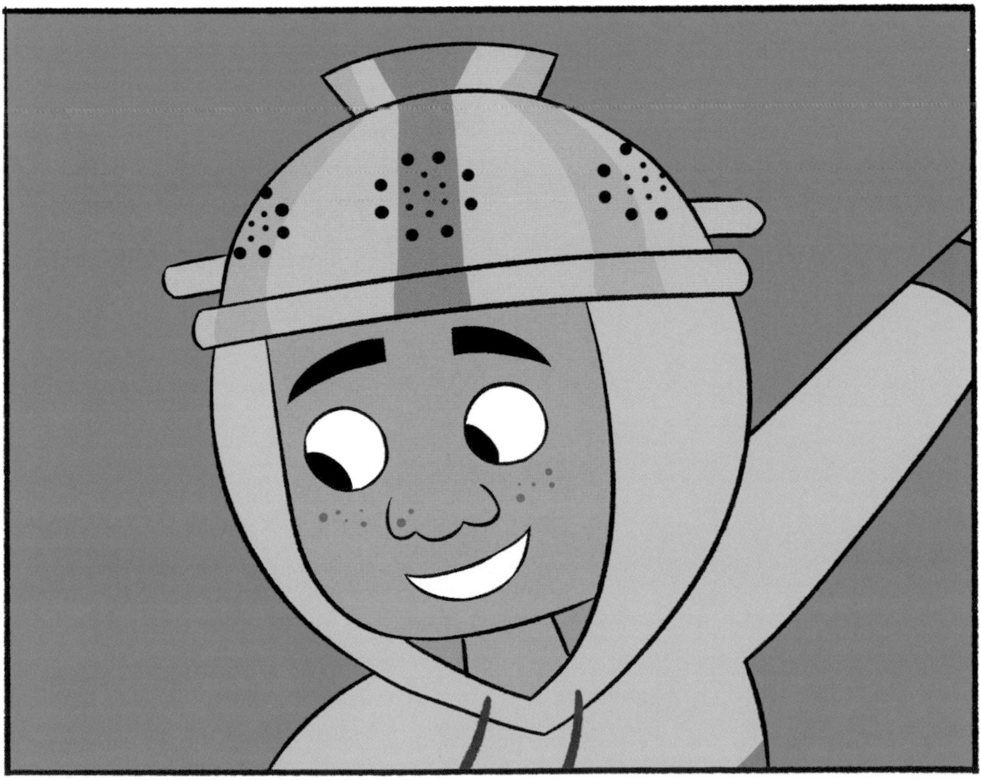

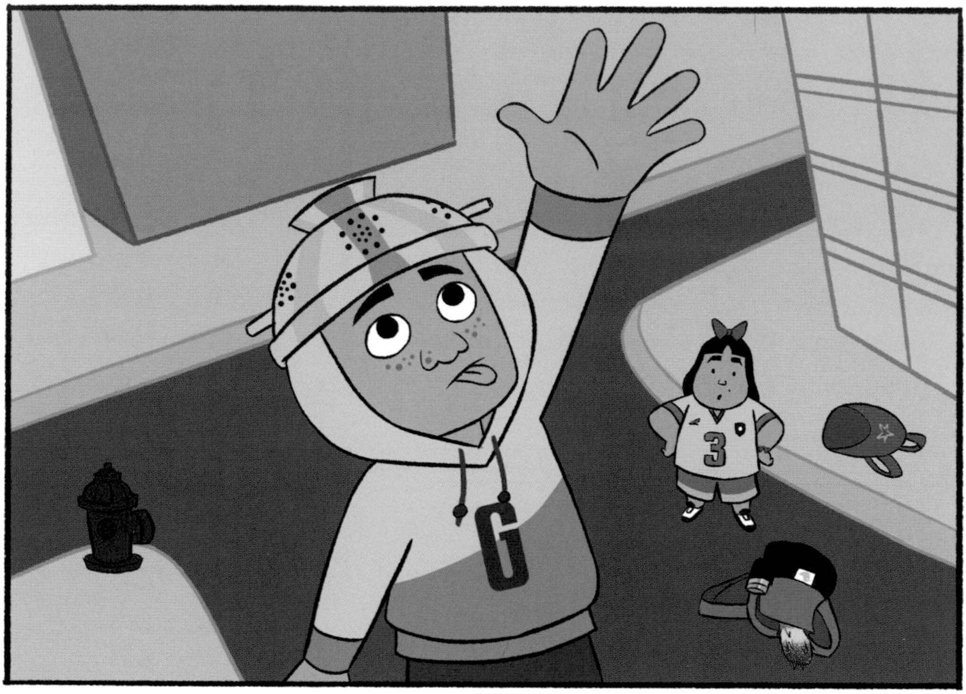

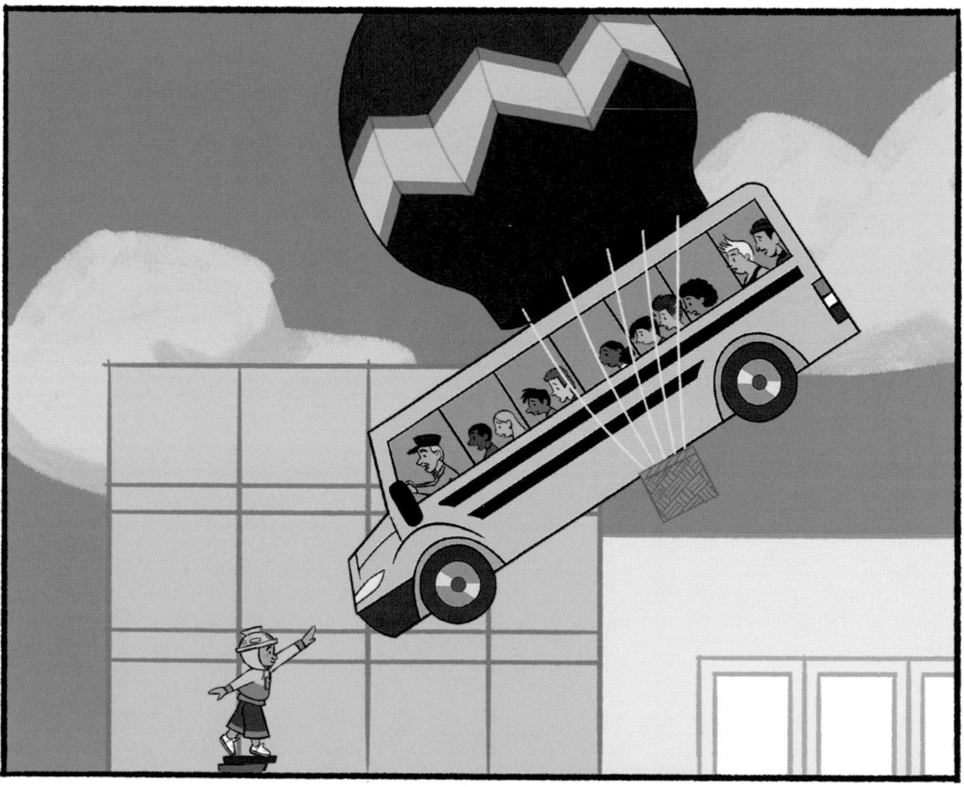

CHAPTER 7: A KAZOO EMERGENCY

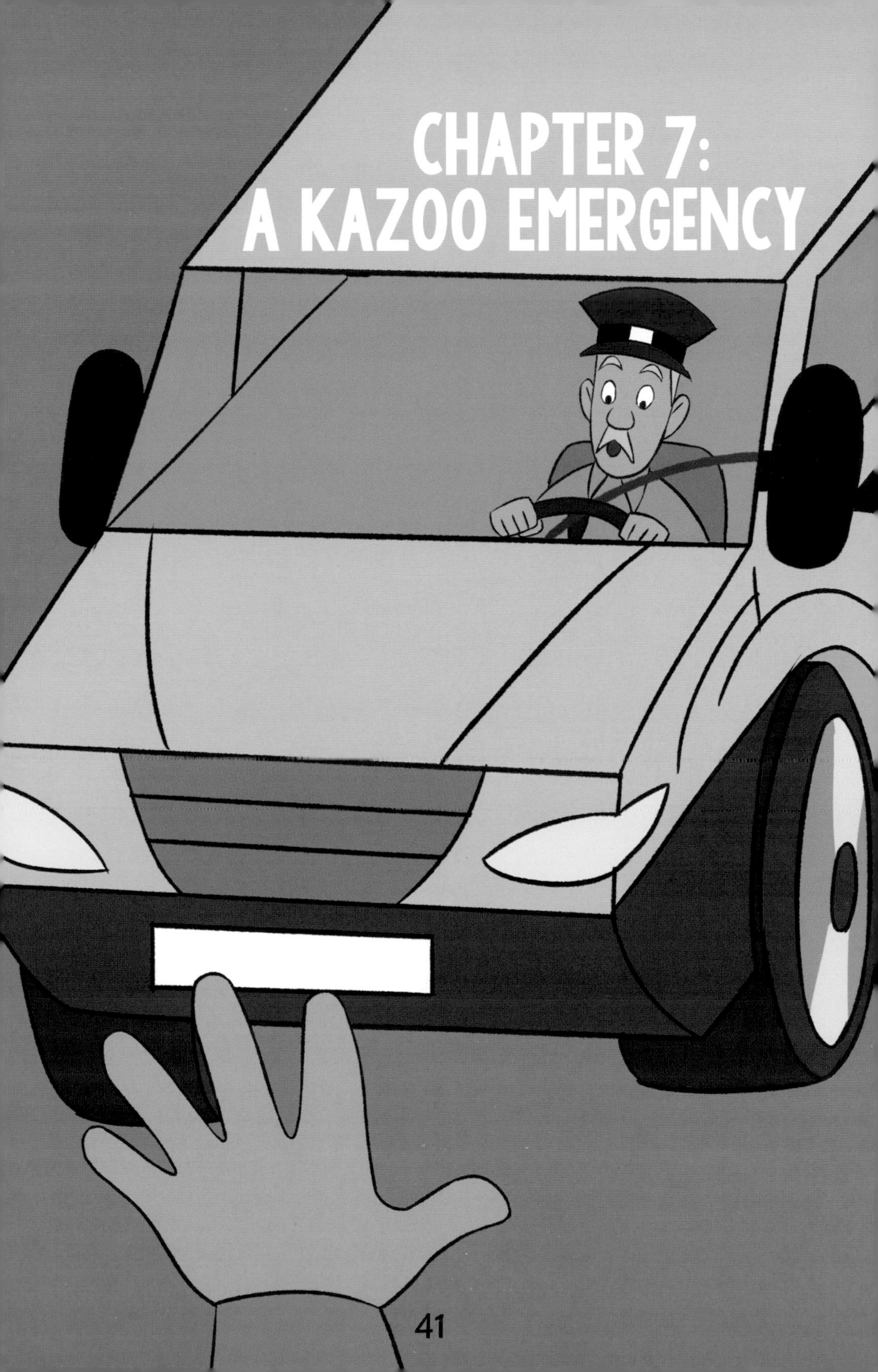

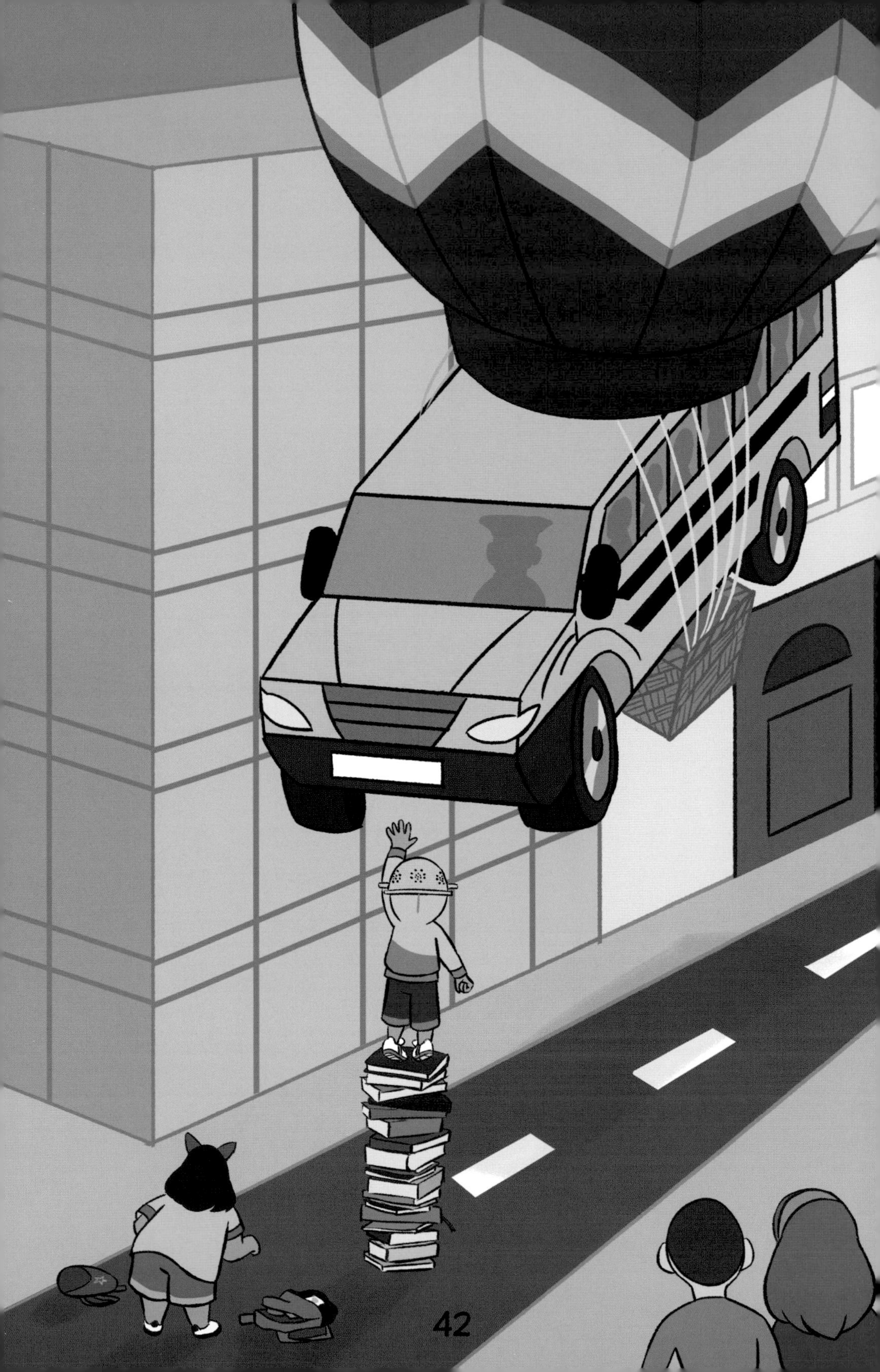

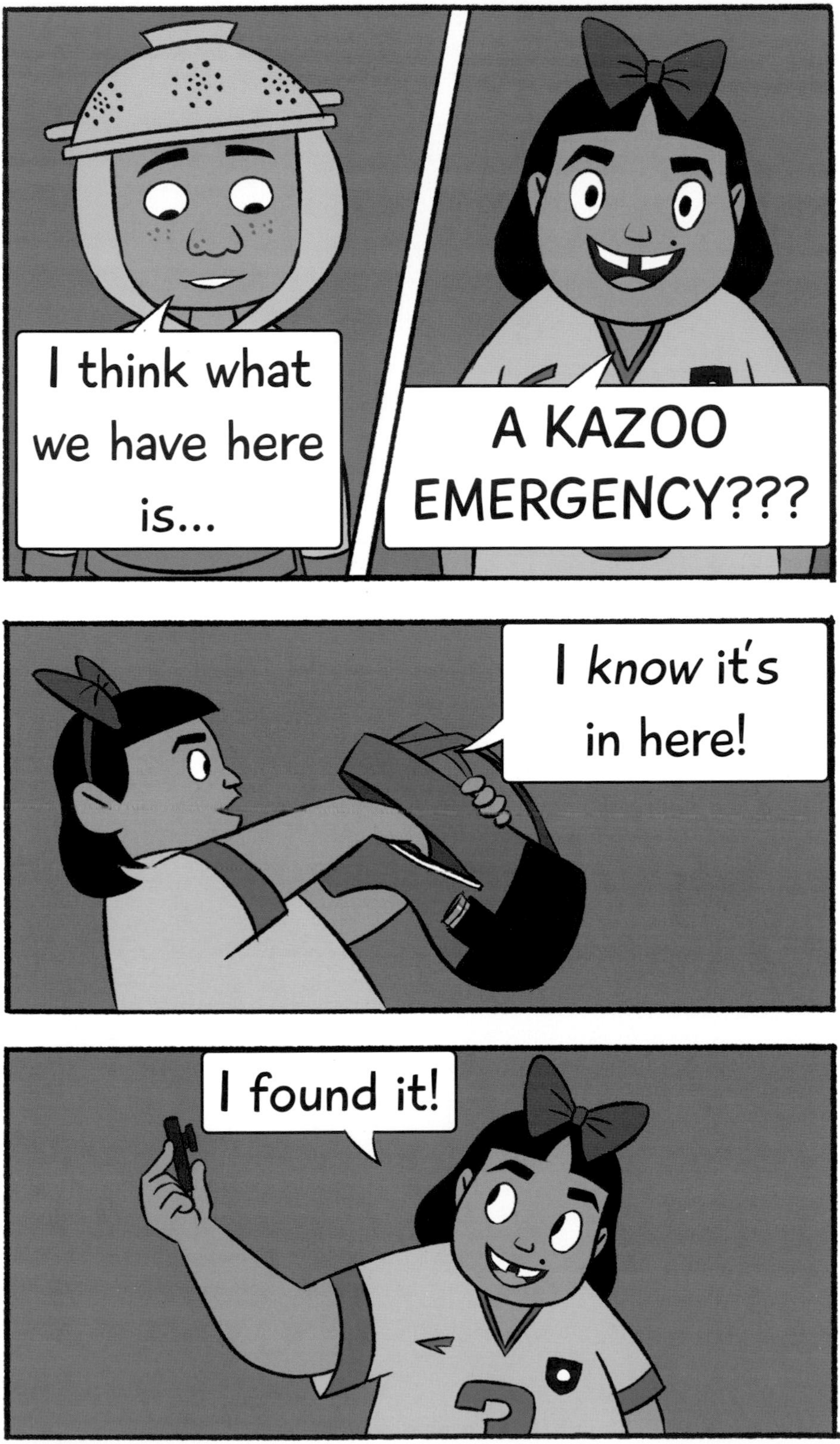
I think what we have here is...
A KAZOO EMERGENCY???
I *know* it's in here!
I found it!

Here it is!

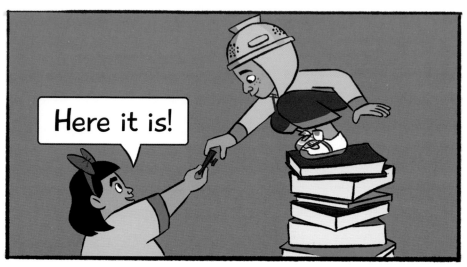

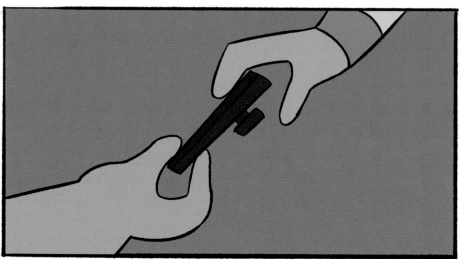

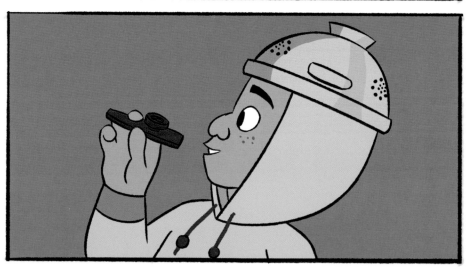

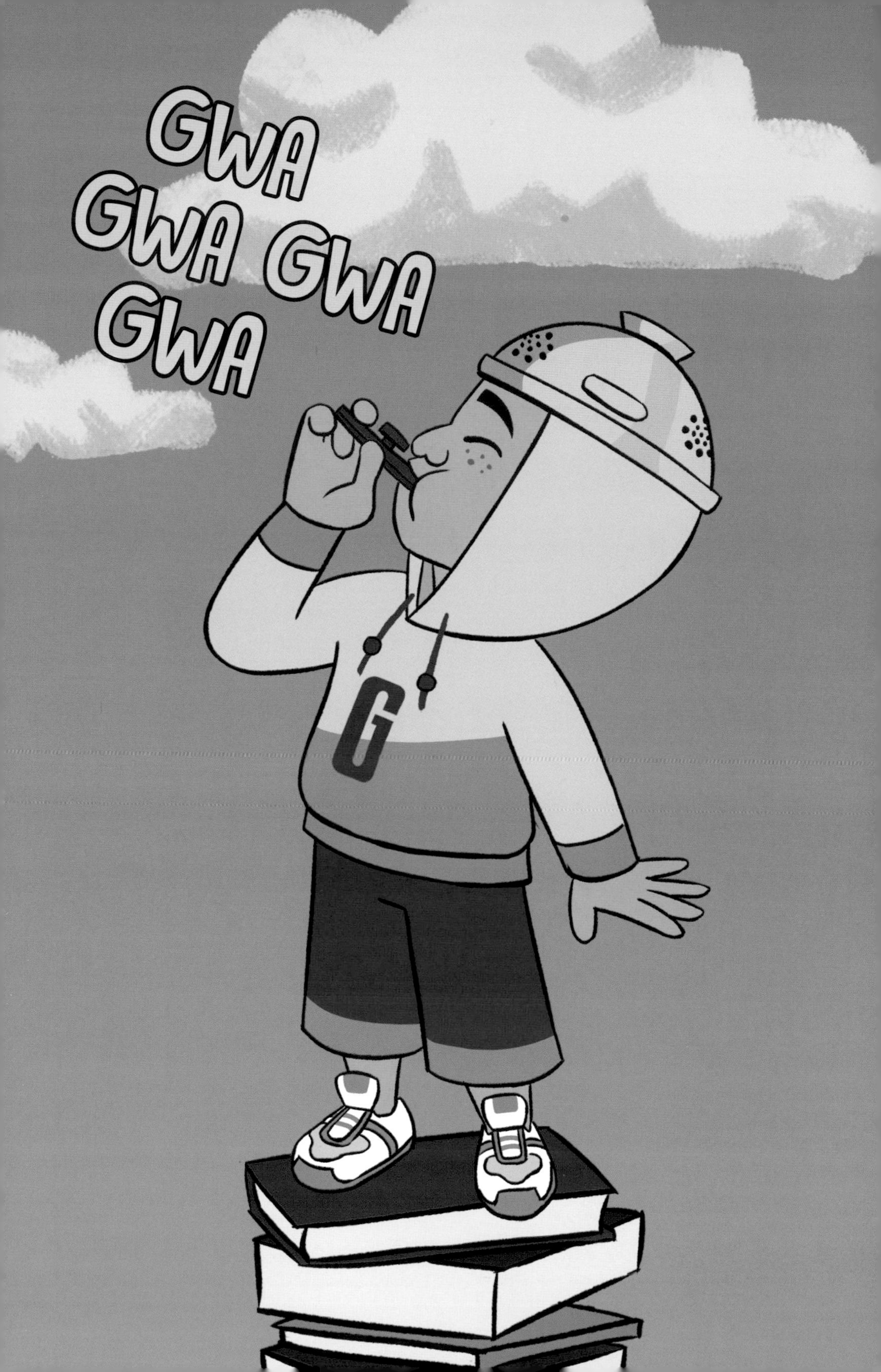
GWA
GWA GWA
GWA

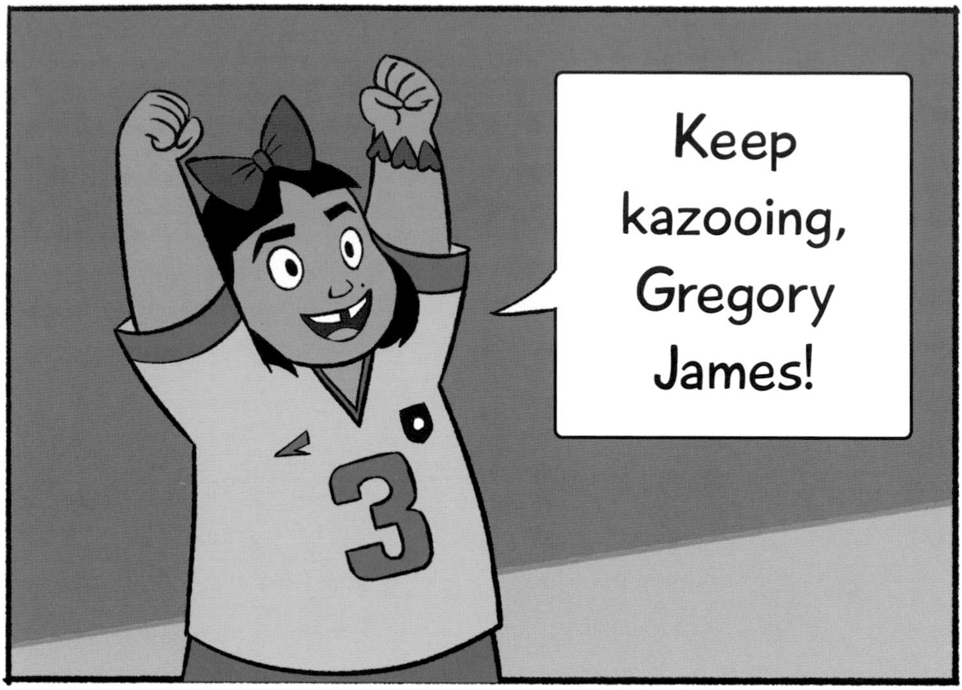
Keep kazooing, Gregory James!

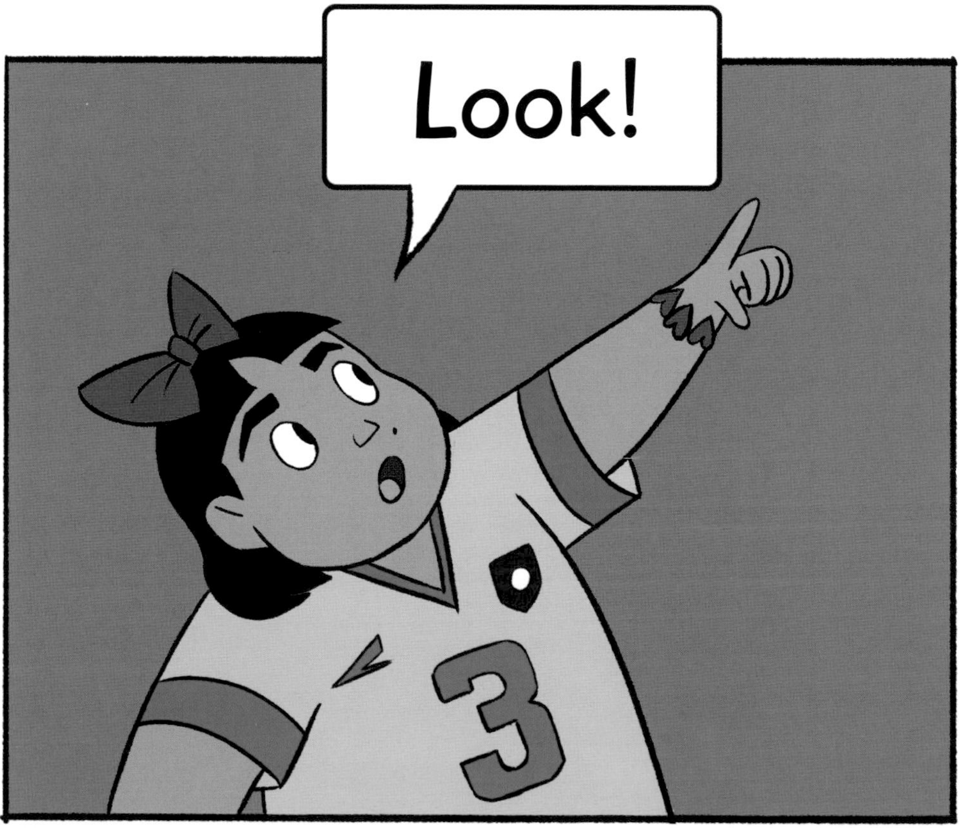
Look!

CHAPTER 8:
GEESE TO THE RESCUE

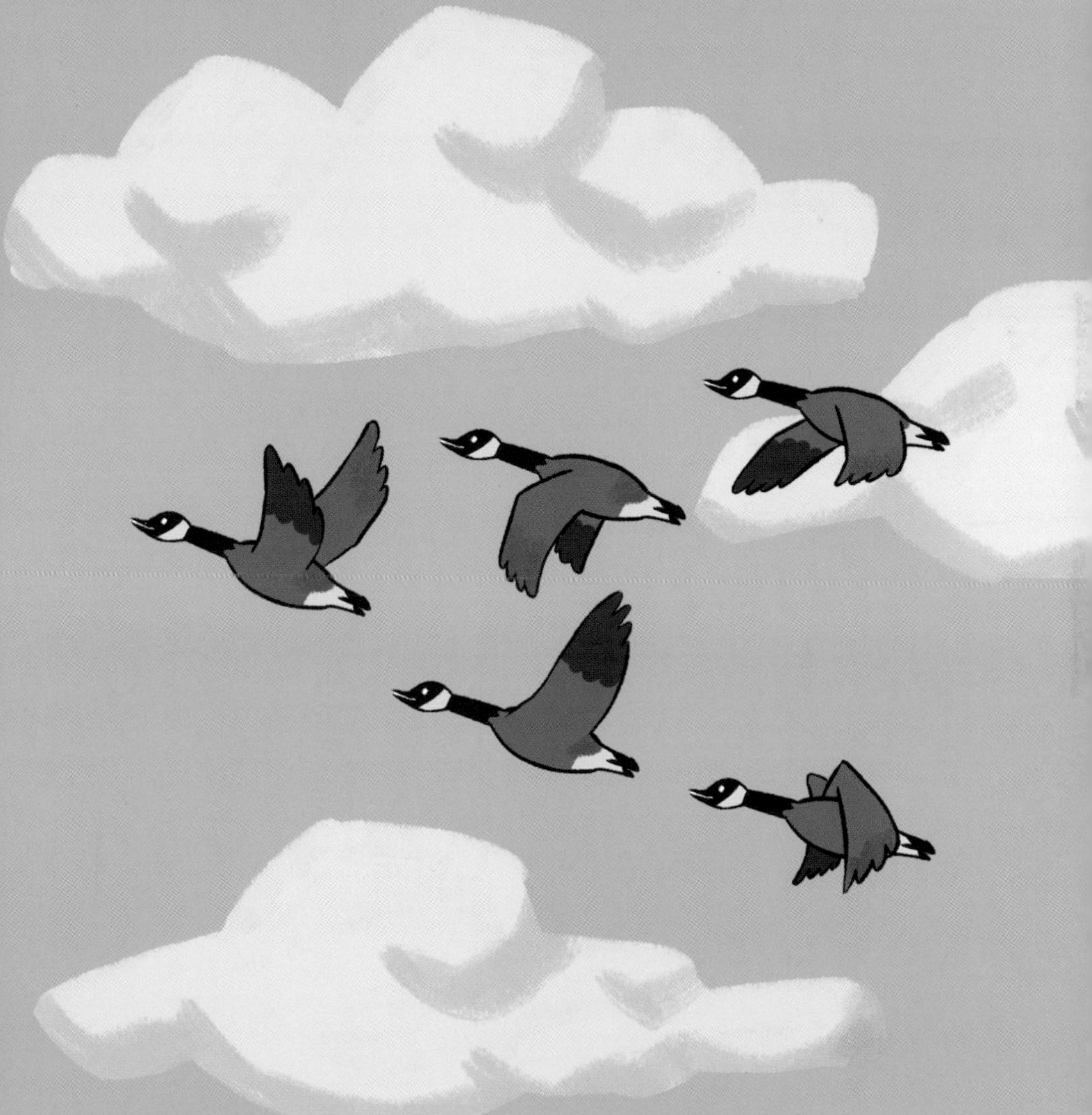

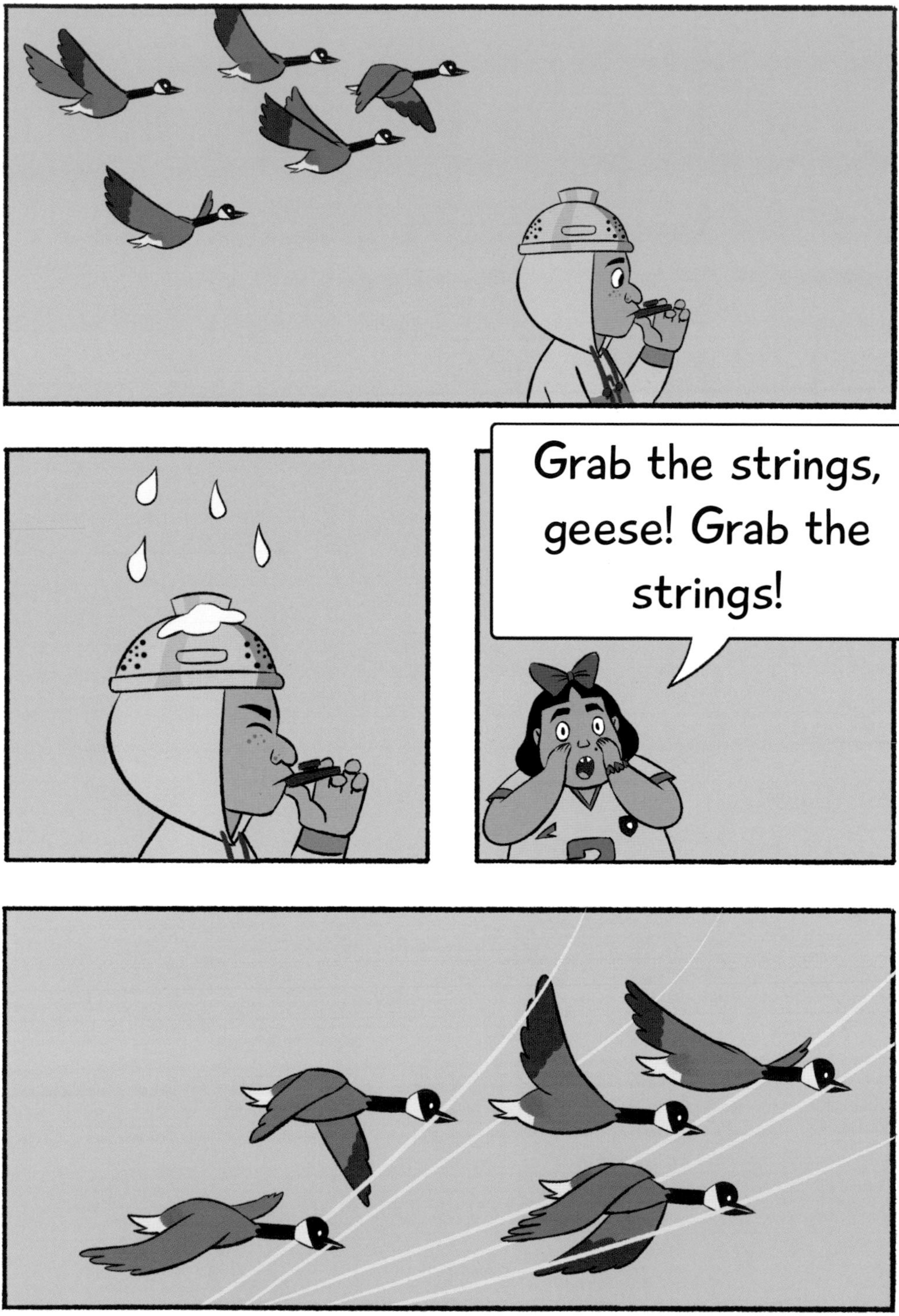
Grab the strings, geese! Grab the strings!

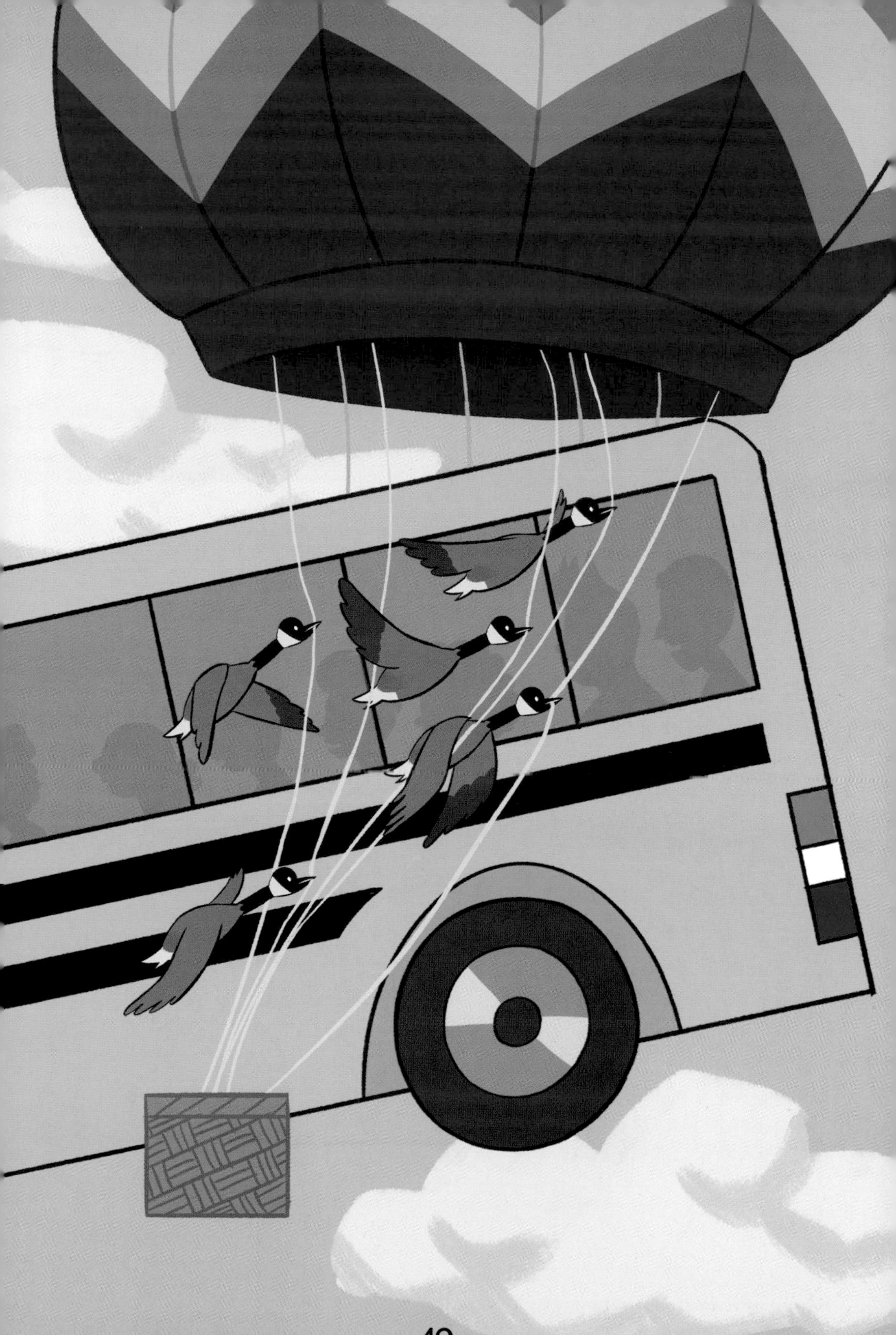

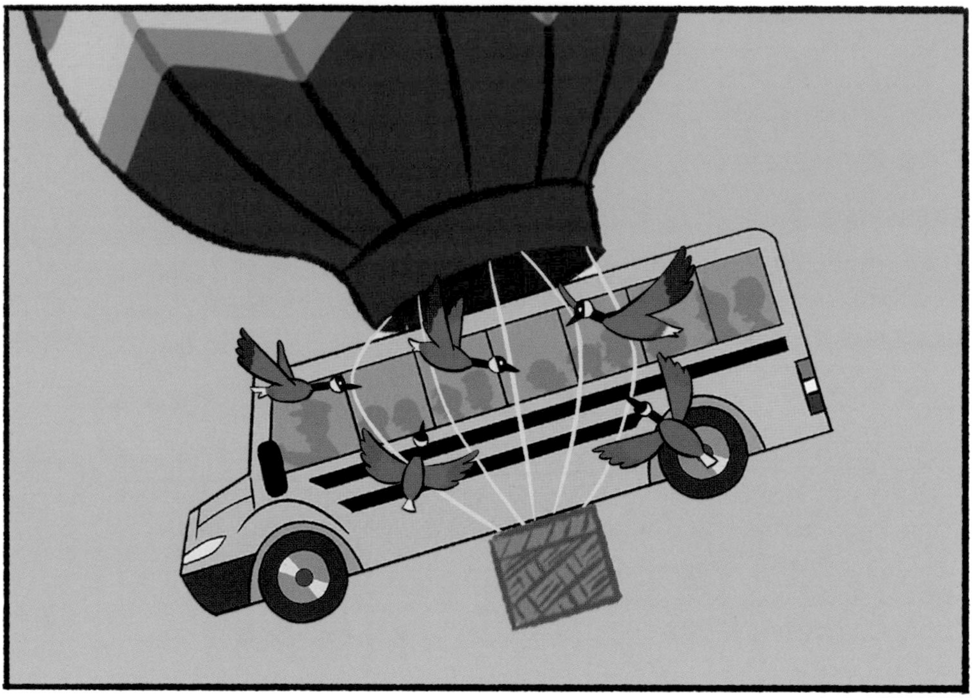

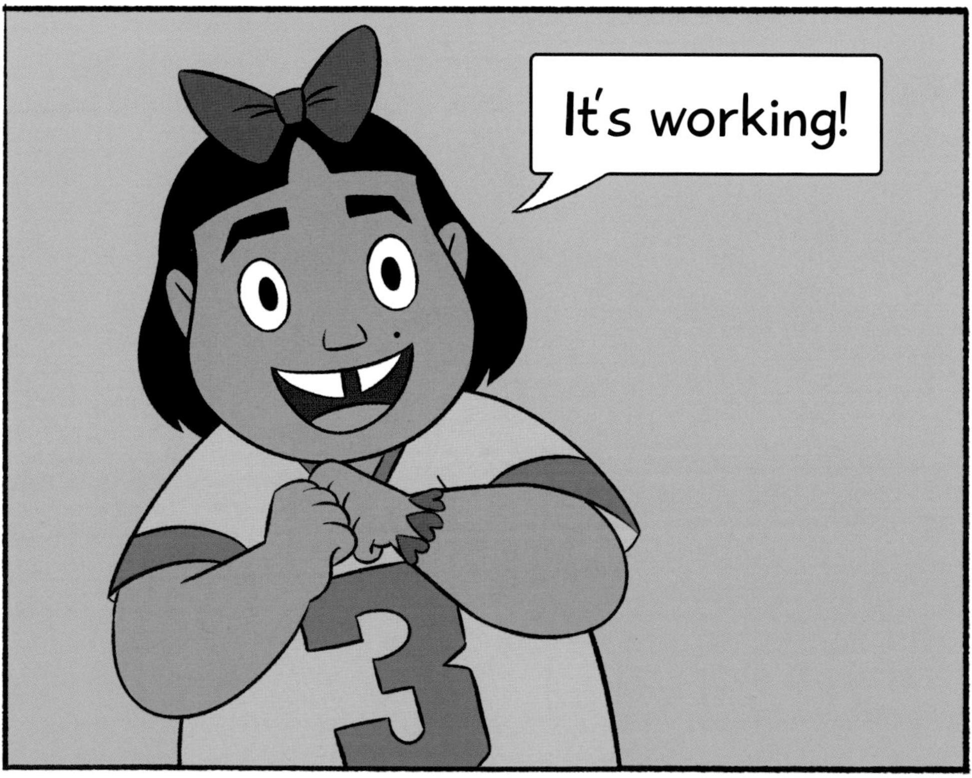
It's working!

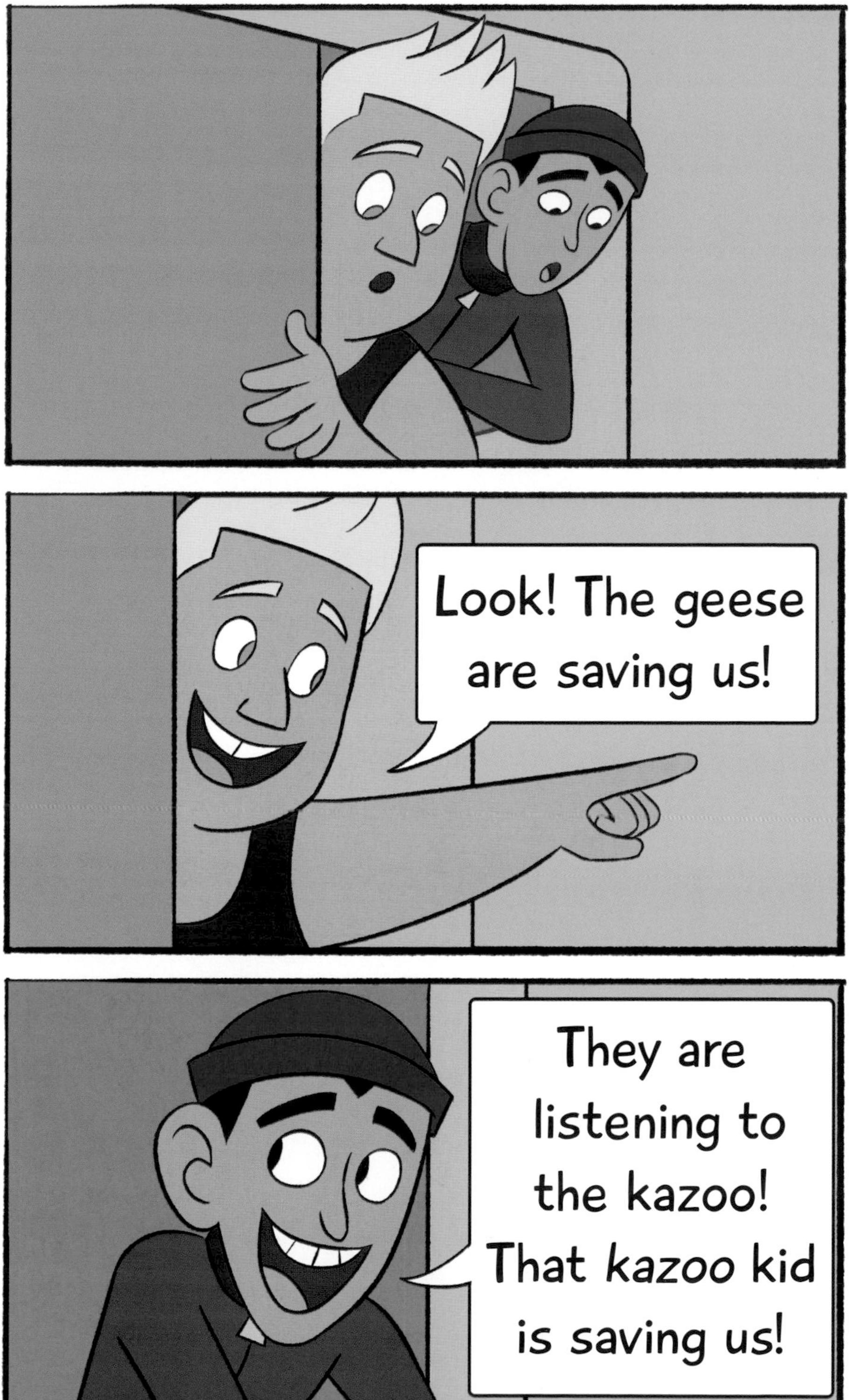

Look! The geese are saving us!
They are listening to the kazoo! That *kazoo* kid is saving us!

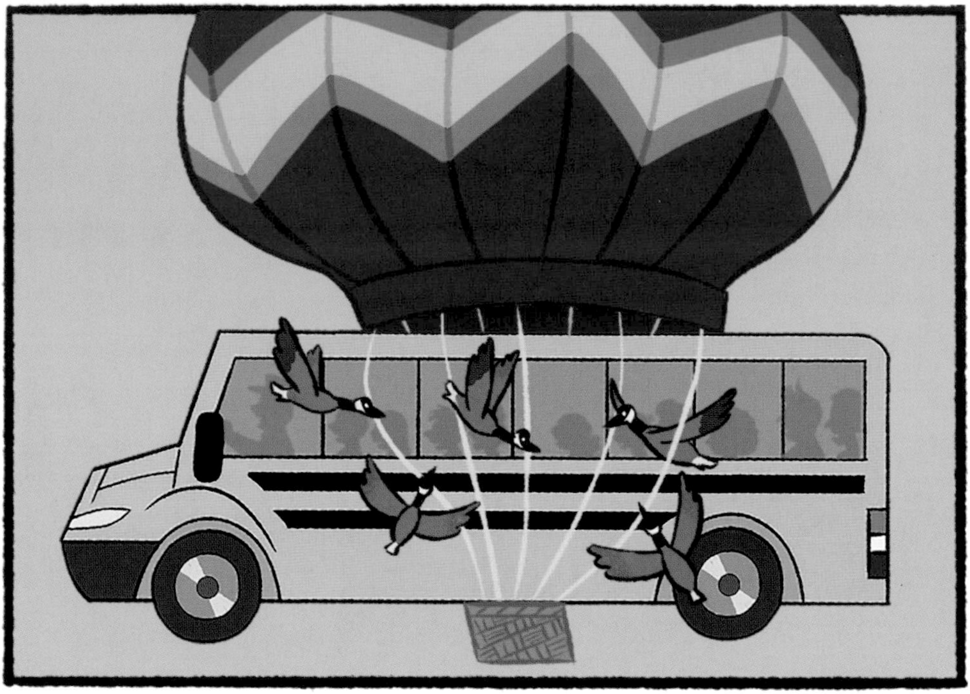

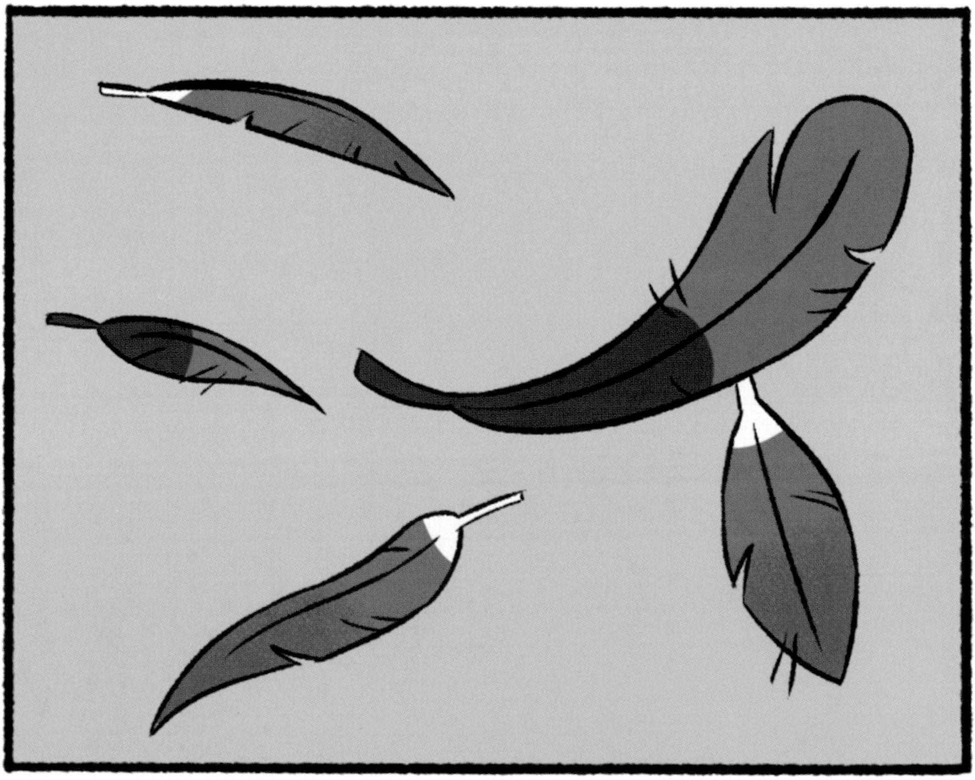

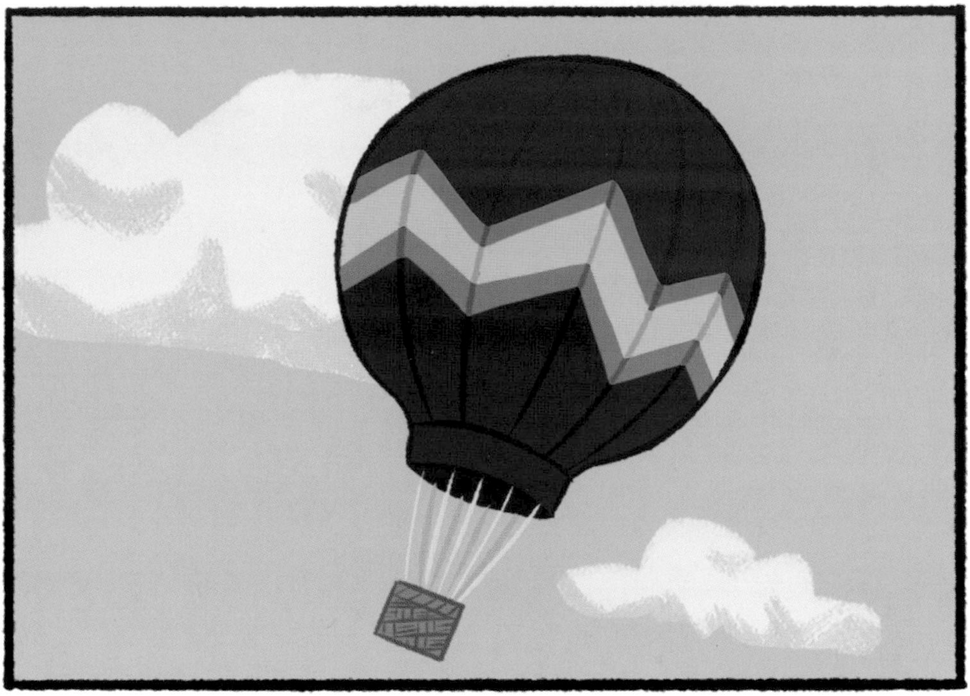

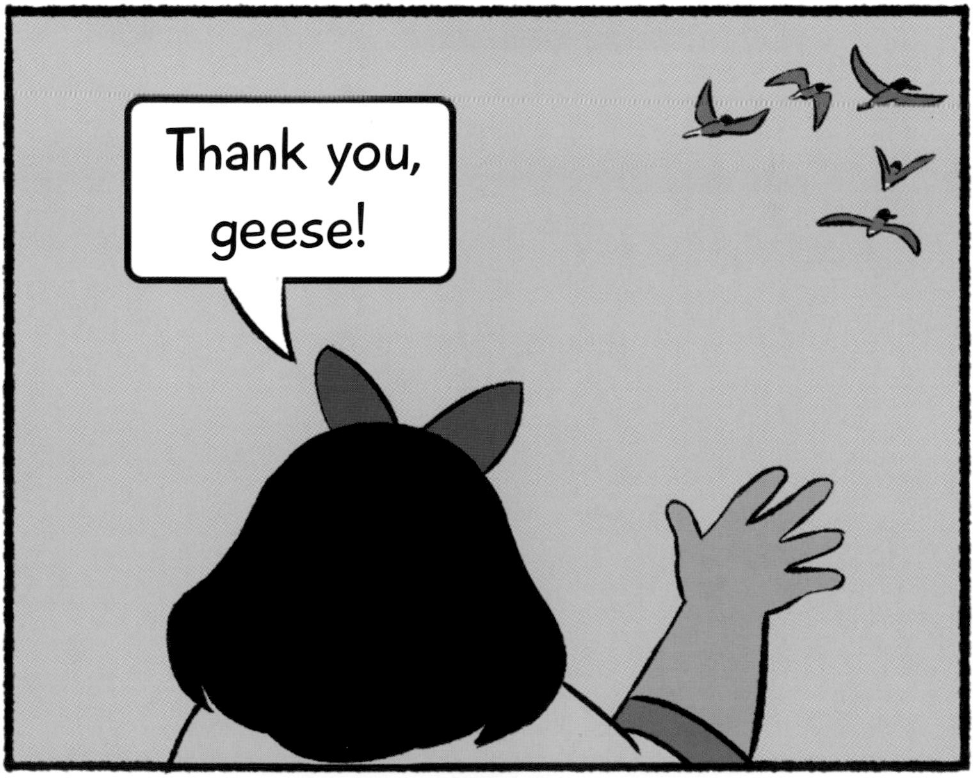
Thank you, geese!

CHAPTER 9: THAT KID SAVED US!

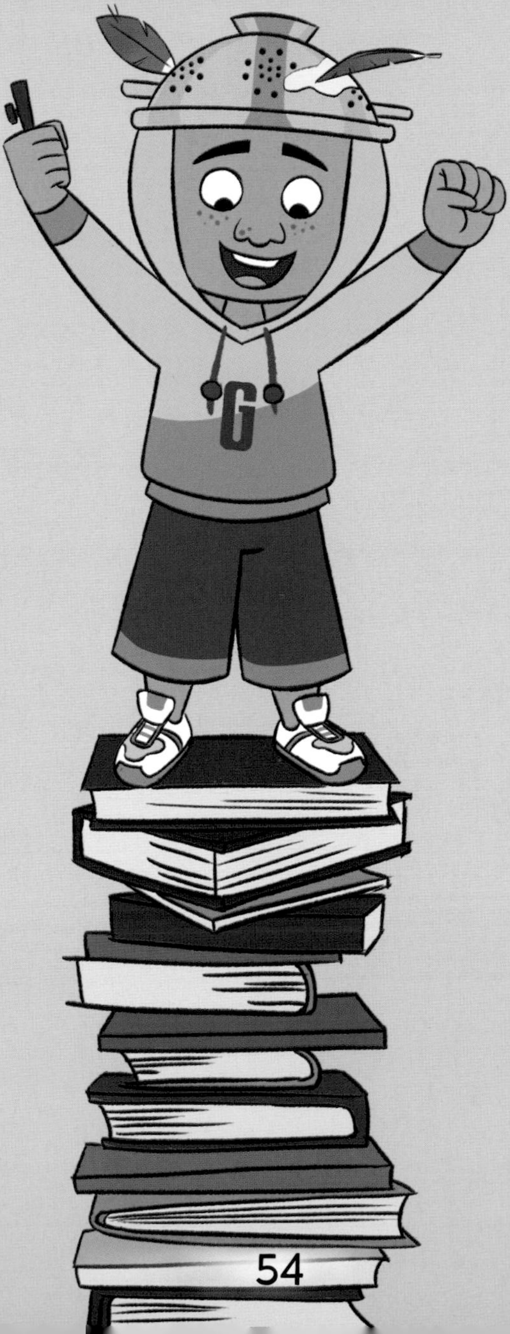

G

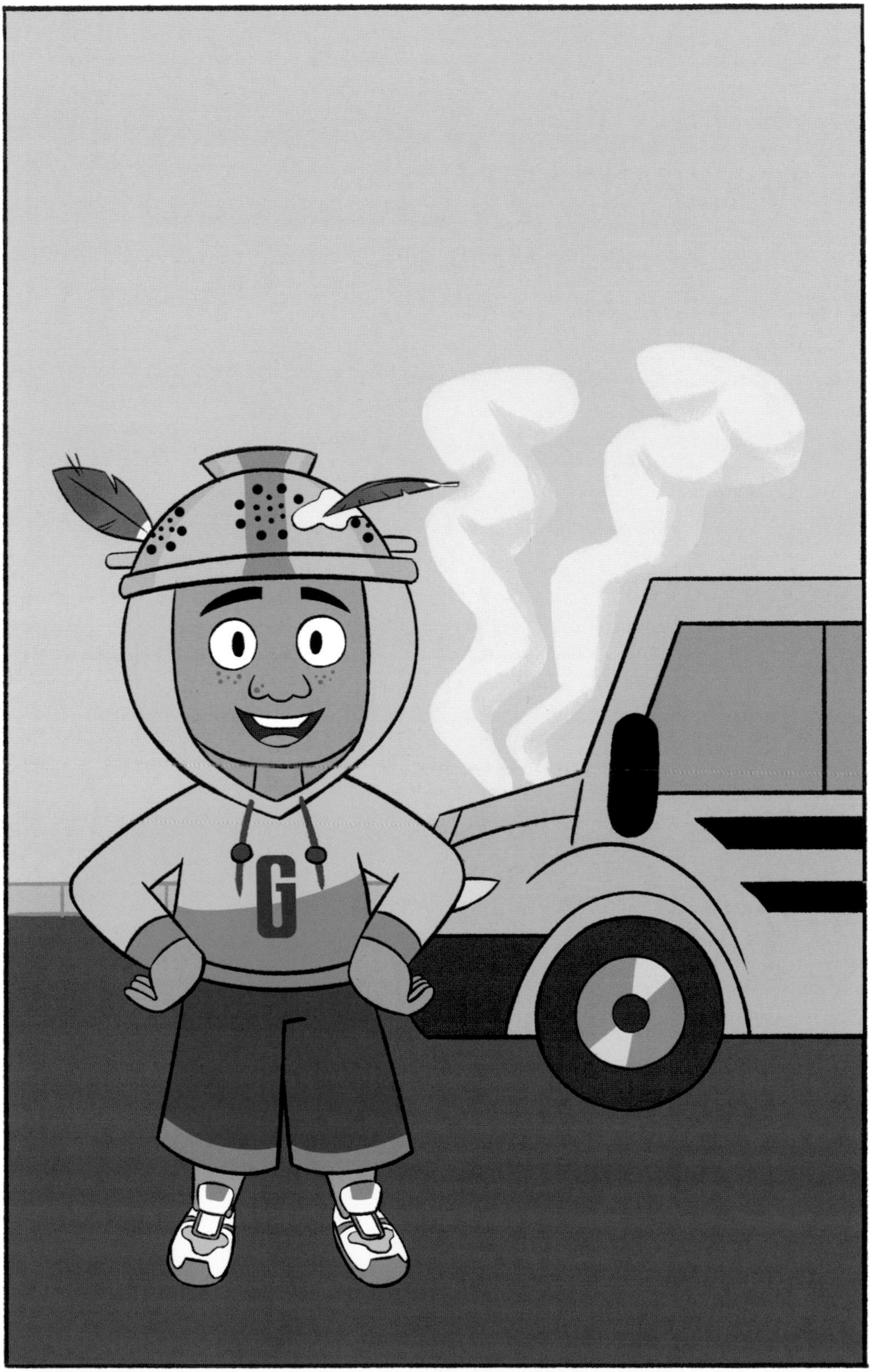
G

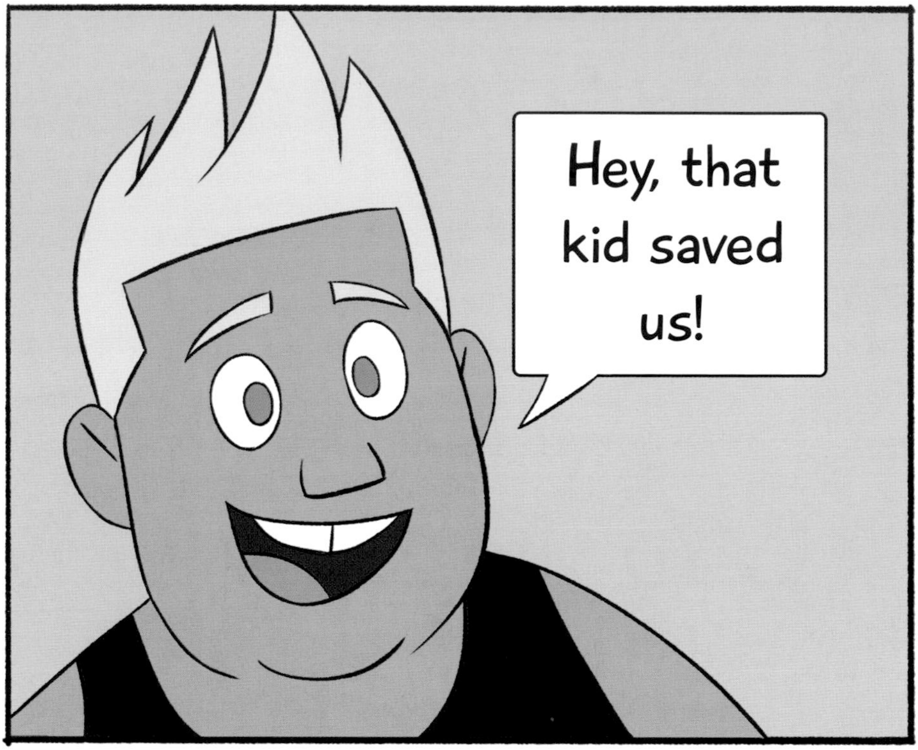
Hey, that kid saved us!

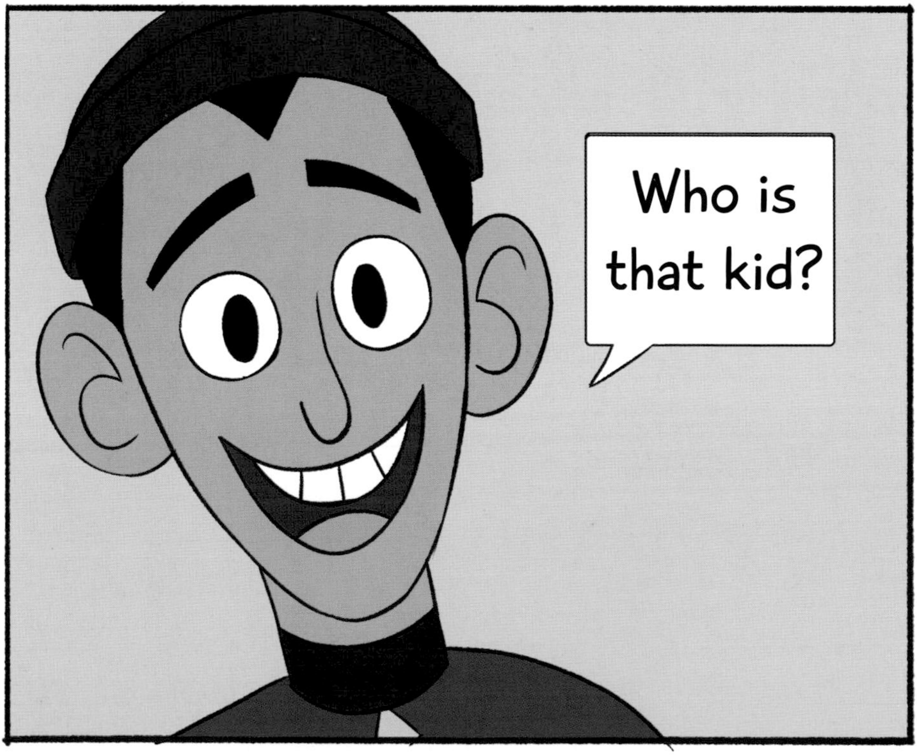
Who is that kid?

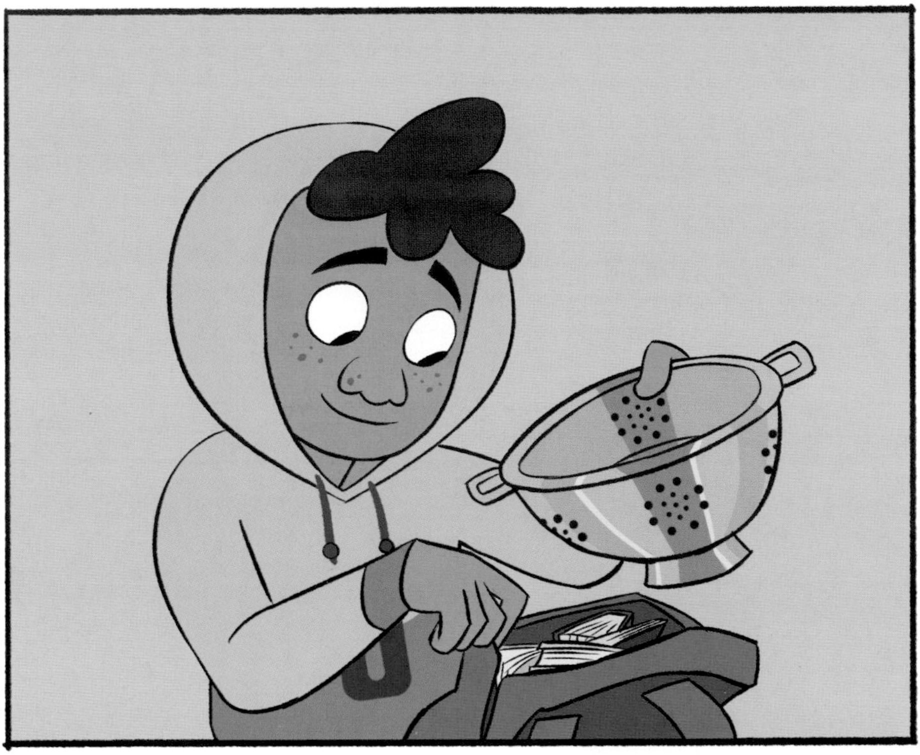

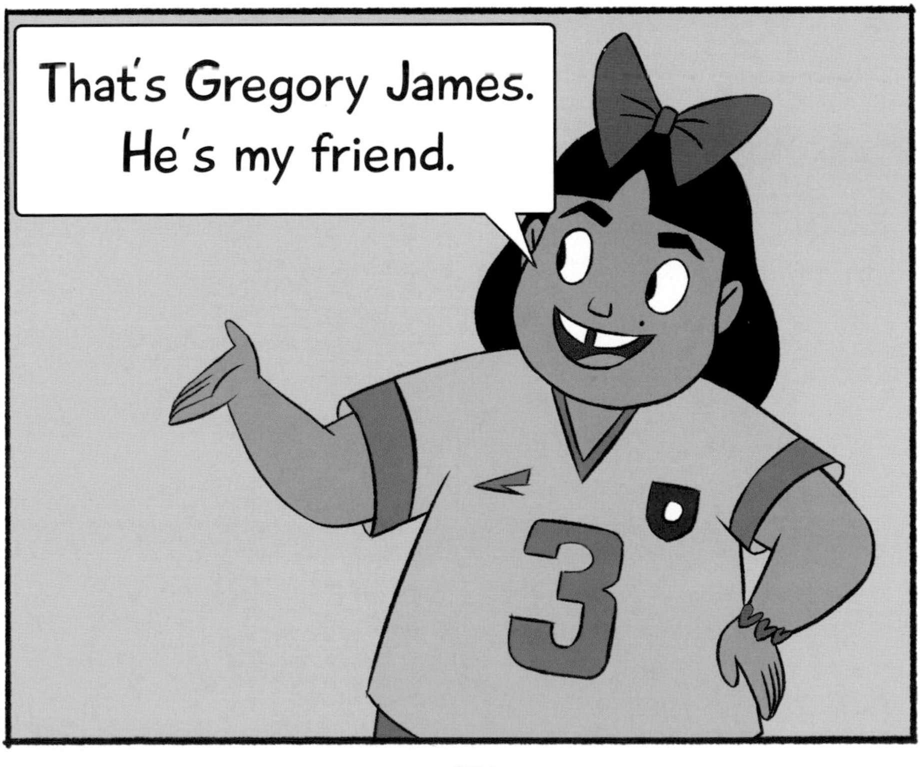
That's Gregory James. He's my friend.

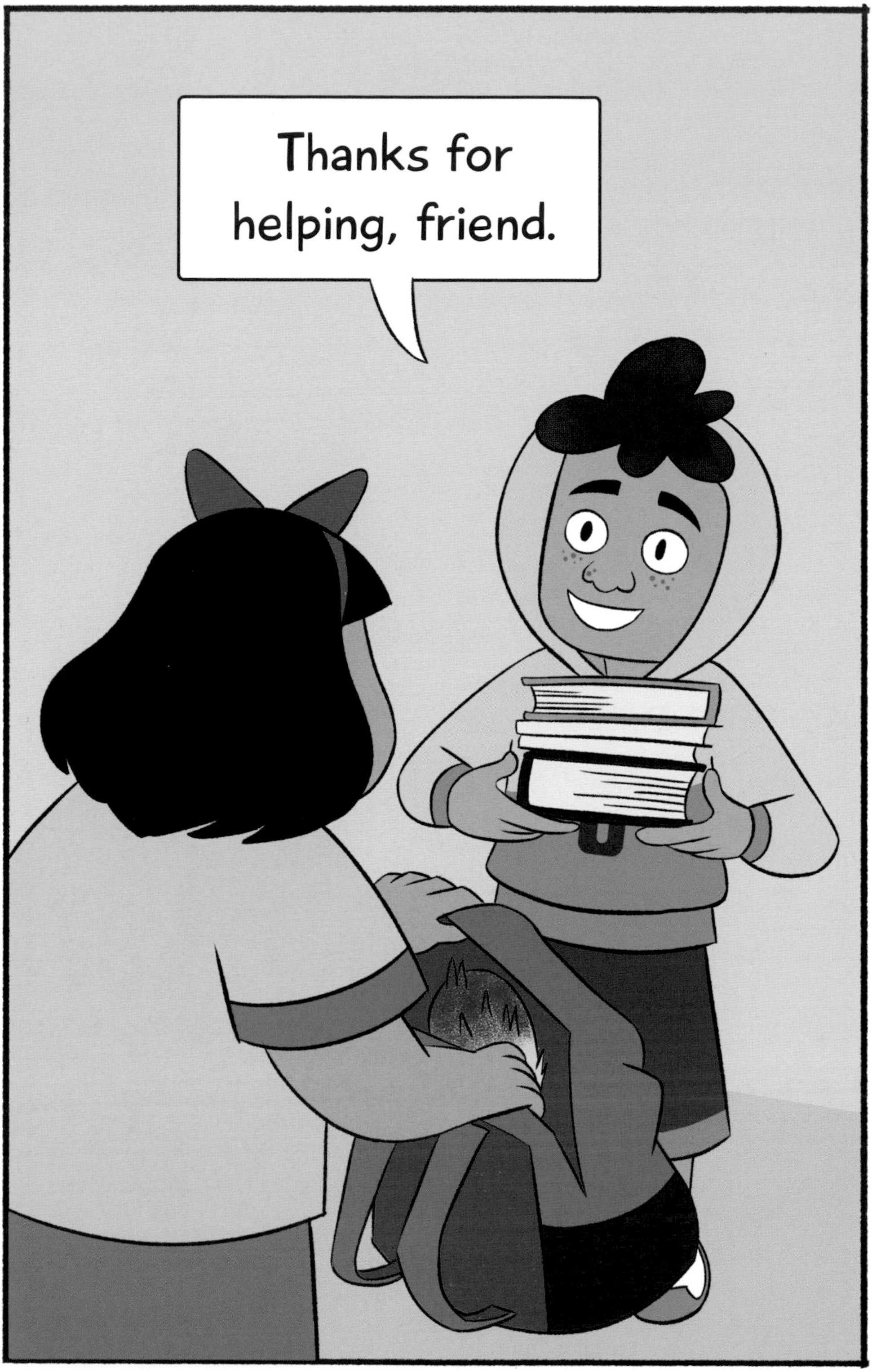
Thanks for helping, friend.

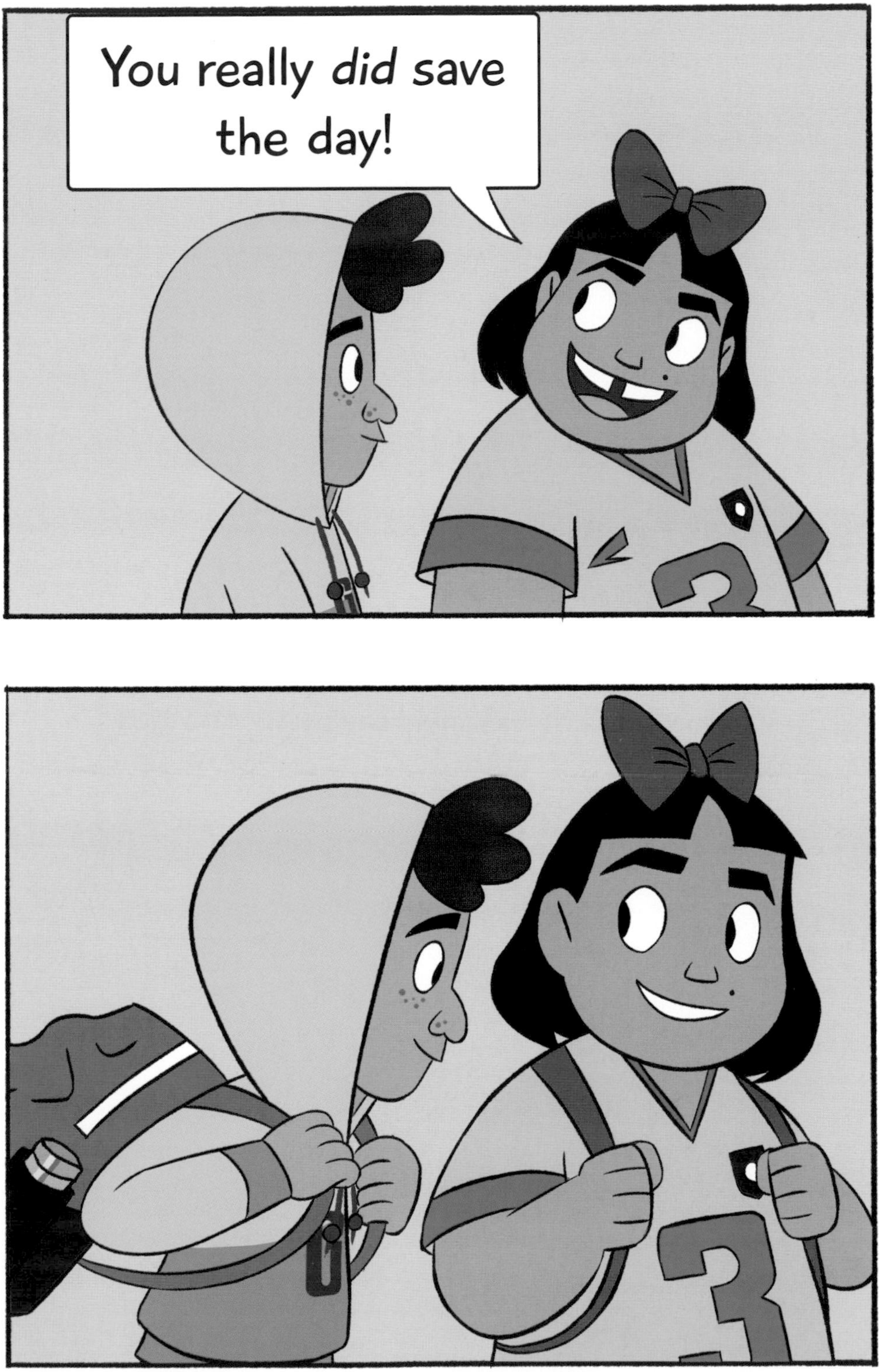
You really *did* save the day!

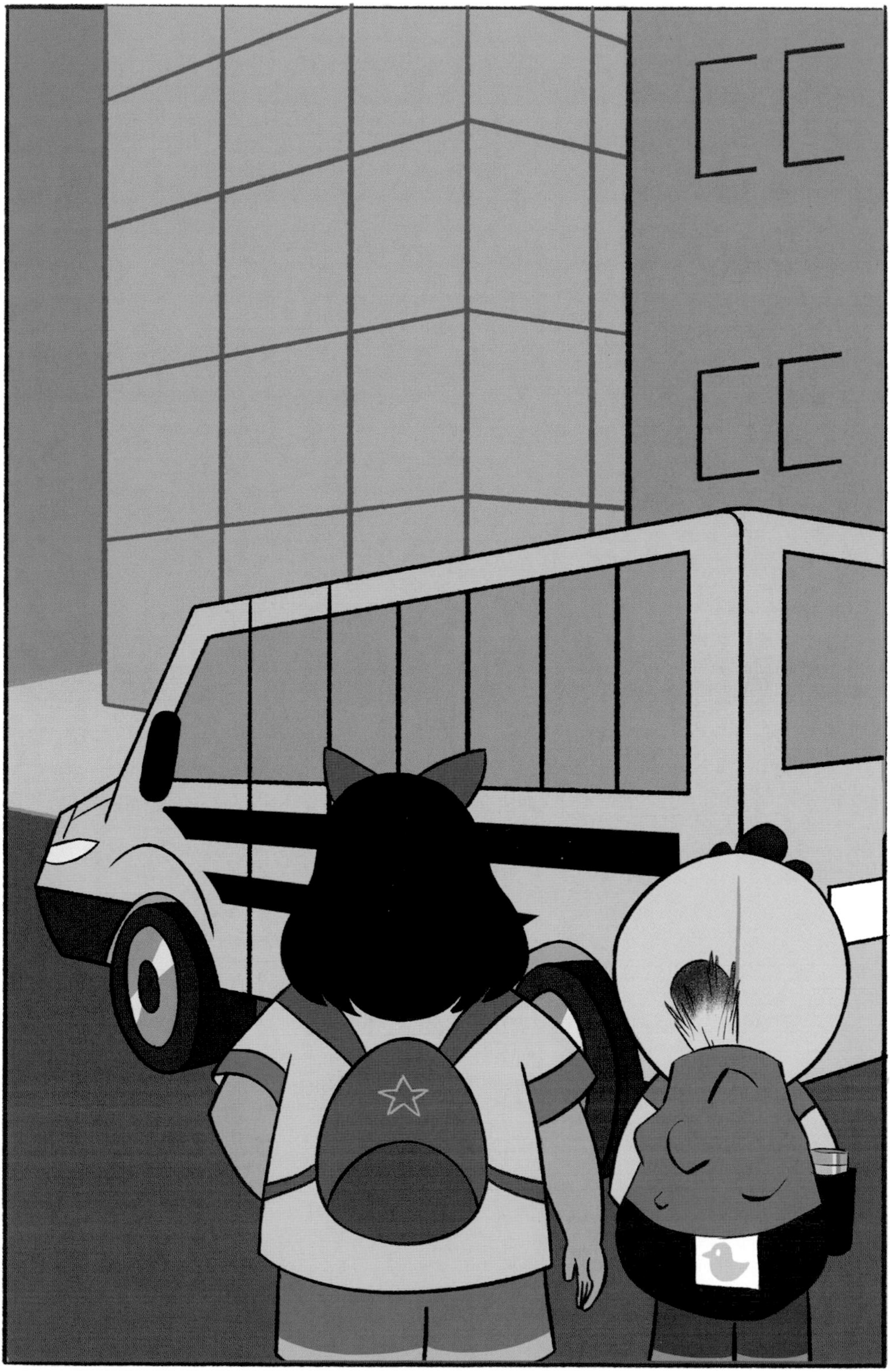

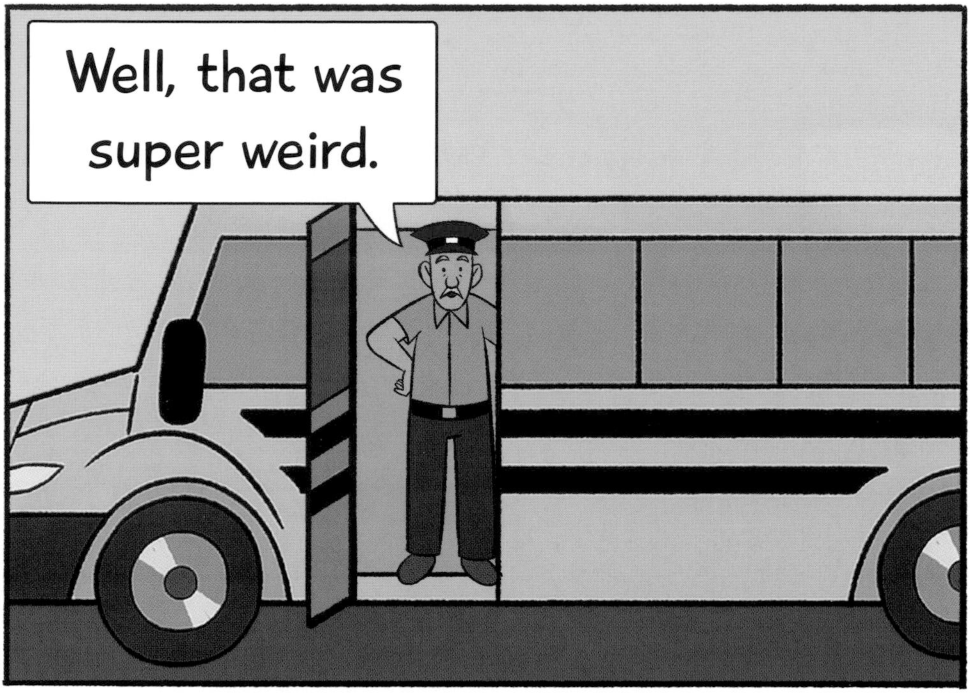
Well, that was super weird.

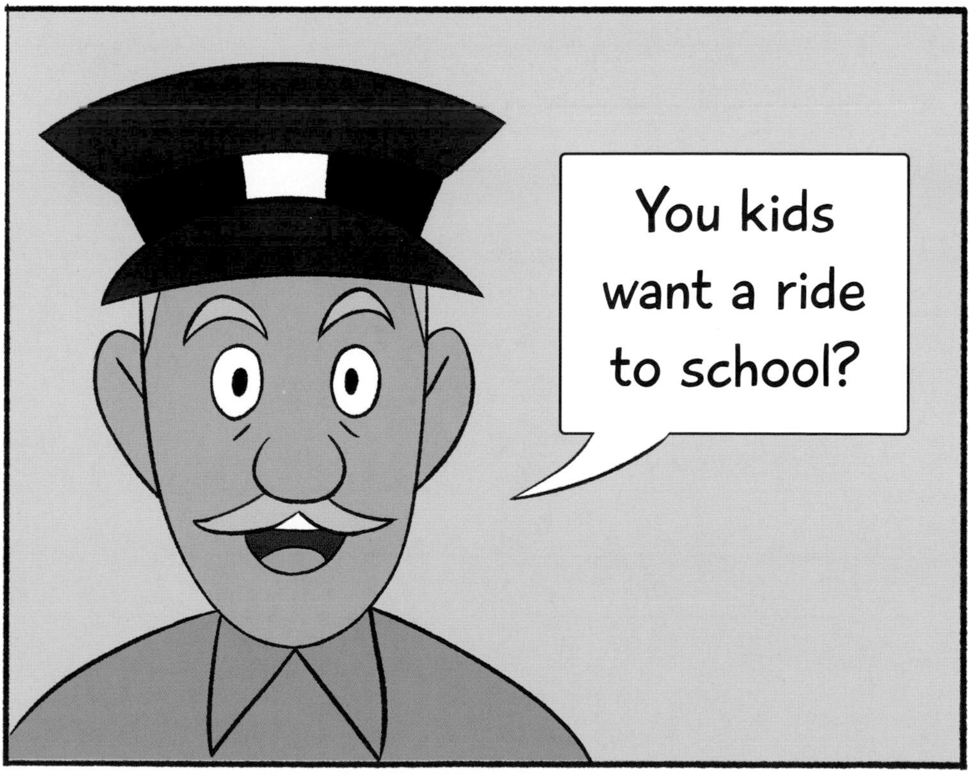
You kids want a ride to school?

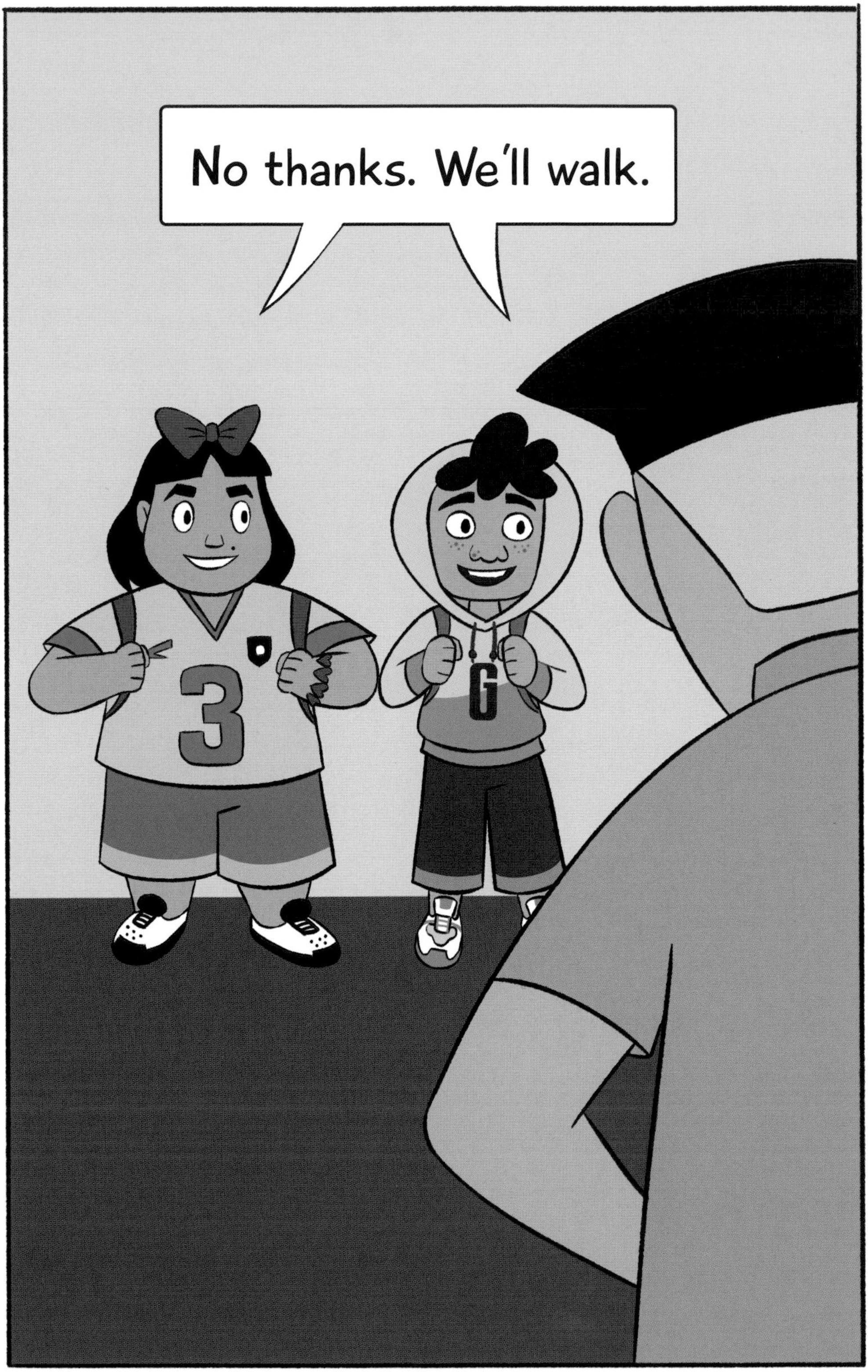
No thanks. We'll walk.

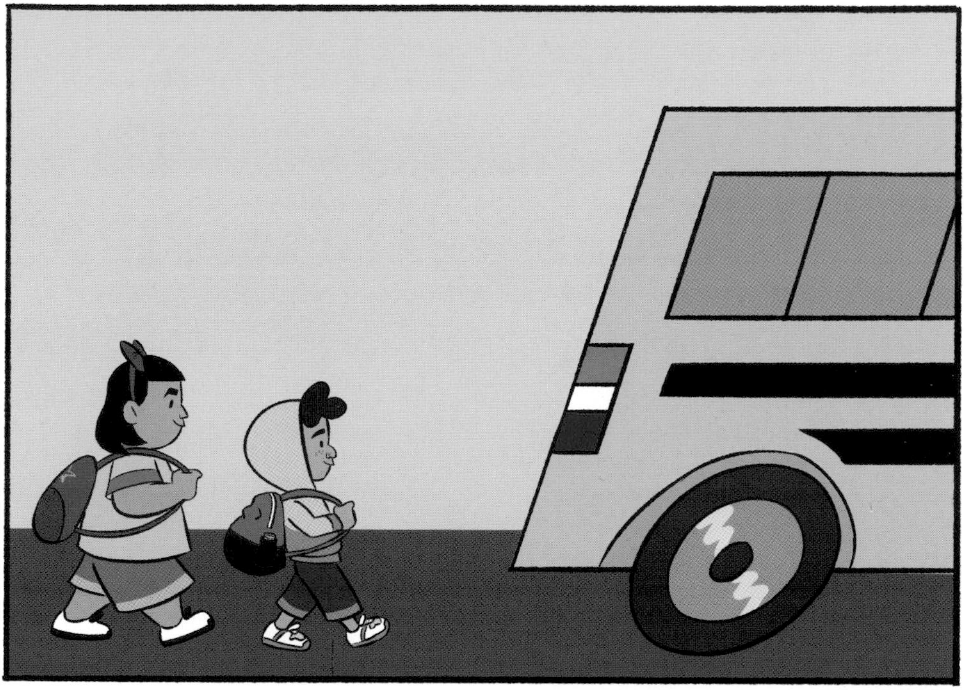

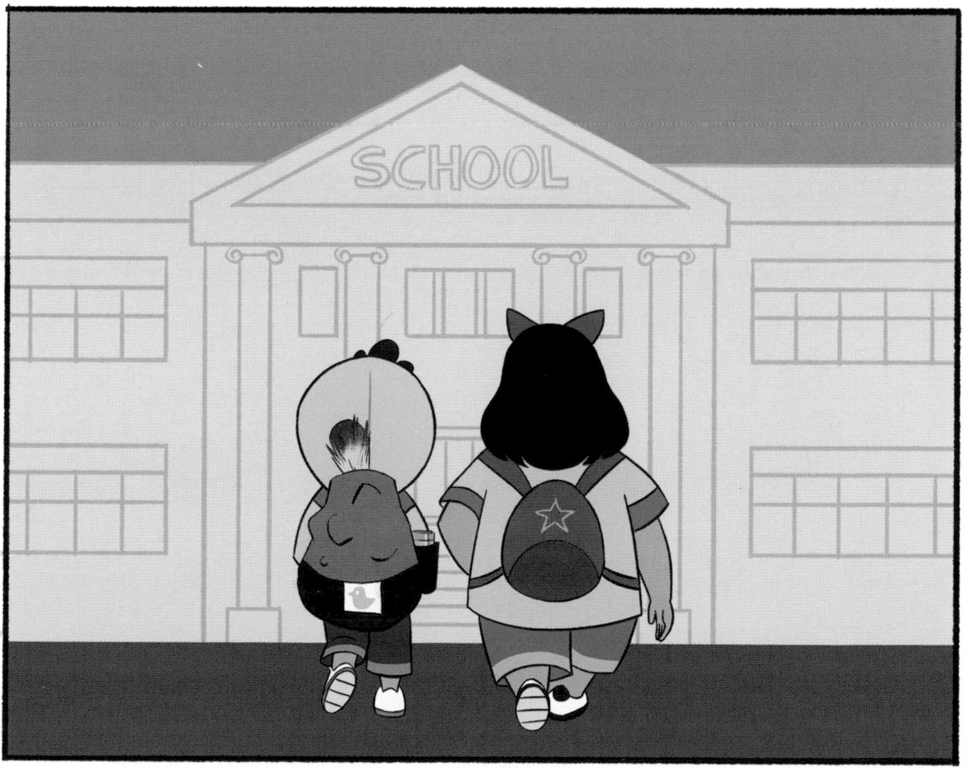
SCHOOL

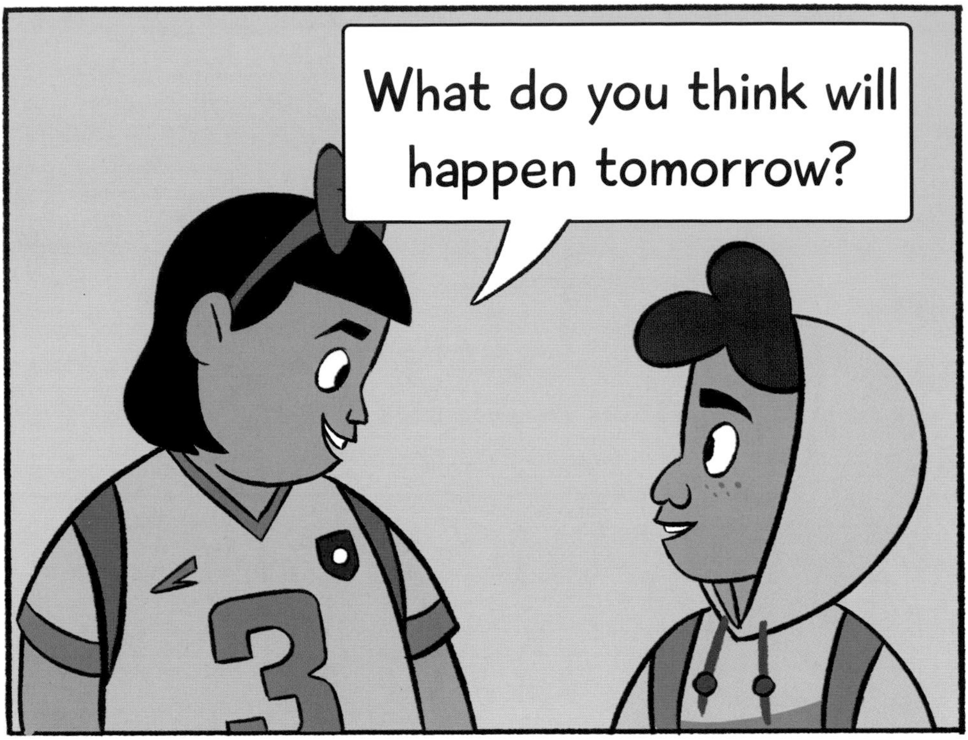
What do you think will happen tomorrow?

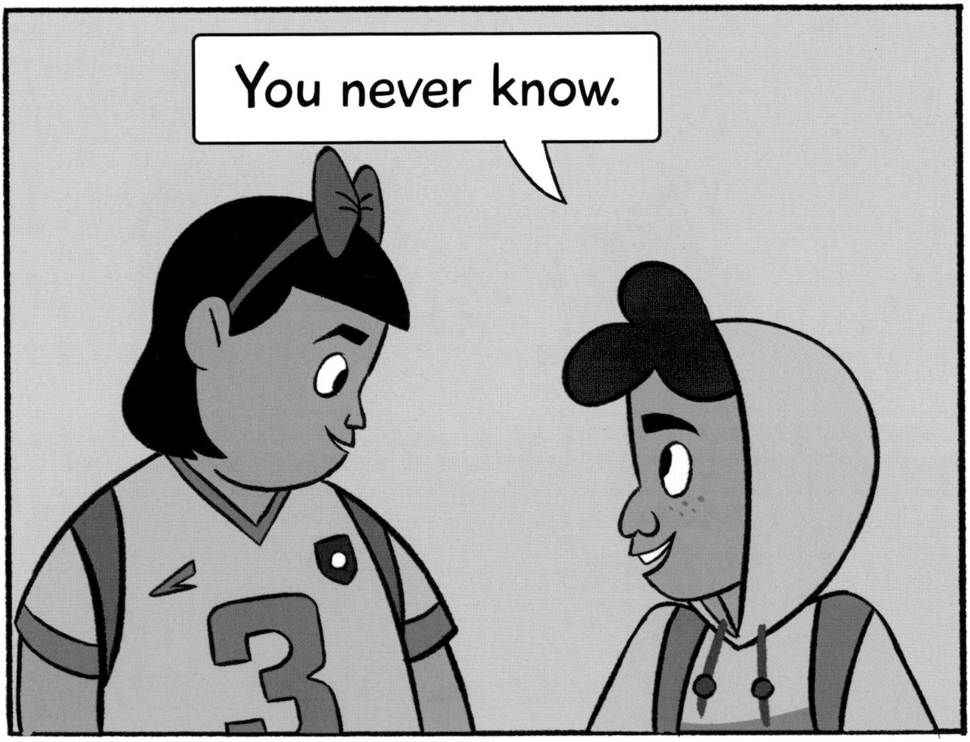
You never know.